"So you asked a guy who ditched us without so much as a good-bye to chaperon us for a month?" Conner demanded, searching his mother's face for some indication that she hadn't gone completely insane.

Mrs. Sandborn shook her head and stared at him soberly. "The point is, you need somebody here. I wasn't about to leave you alone and have the Department of Human Services take me to court for being a negligent parent."

"If they haven't prosecuted you yet, I doubt this little vacation would change their minds," Conner said.

Mrs. Sandborn drew back, her face so flushed with anger, it was almost the same color as her scarlet blouse. She shook her head slowly, her eyes riveted on his, then dropped her chin and began muttering something under her breath. It sounded like she was counting.

"Look, Conner," Mrs. Sandborn said finally, taking a deep breath and rubbing her hand over her forehead. "I can't deal with this right now. Gary is Megan's father, and he's staying here while I'm gone."

"Then I guess I'll be looking for a place to stay," Conner uttered through clenched teeth.

Don't miss any of the books in SWEET VALLEY HIGH
SENIOR YEAR, an exciting series from Bantam Books!

Visit the Official Sweet Valley Web Site on the Internet at:

http://www.sweetvalley.com

Francine Pascal's SVH senioryear

Take Me On

CREATED BY
FRANCINE PASCAL

BANTAM BOOKS
NEW YORK · TORONTO · LONDON · SYDNEY · AUCKLAND

RL 6, age 12 and up

TAKE ME ON

A Bantam Book / December 1999

Sweet Valley High® is a registered trademark of Francine Pascal.
Conceived by Francine Pascal.
Cover photography by Michael Segal.

Produced by 17th Street Productions,
a division of Daniel Weiss Associates, Inc.
33 West 17th Street
New York, NY 10011.

ISBN: 0-553-49283-7

Published simultaneously in the United States and Canada

Bantam Books are published by Bantam Books, a division of Random
House, Inc. Its trademark, consisting of the words "Bantam Books" and
the portrayal of a rooster, is Registered in U.S. Patent and Trademark
Office and in other countries. Marca Registrada. Bantam Books, 1540
Broadway, New York, New York 10036.

PRINTED IN THE UNITED STATES OF AMERICA

OPM   0 9 8 7 6 5 4 3 2 1

To Vilma Banos

Jessica Wakefield

Okay, so I kissed Will. So? It was just a fluke, right? One harmless little kiss that lasted for like five seconds, tops. But if it was nothing, why can't I stop thinking about it?

I keep seeing his face, inches away from mine, with that intense look in his gorgeous blue-gray eyes — the look that had me breathing heavy before he even touched me. And then when he kissed me . . . wow. First it was hard, like he couldn't control himself, and then it was soft and sweet as he traced the line of my jaw with his hand. It was like he was studying my face, memorizing it. Then he slid his fingers behind my neck and up through my hair, which was just —

I have to stop obsessing over this — over him. And I will.

As soon as I catch my breath.

Conner McDermott

AP English
Mr. Collins

Question #4: In communication, there is often a disparity between what a person says and how others hear it. Using the passages handed out in class or quotes of your own, show how even simple messages can be interpreted in more than one way. Give at least three examples.

There are two sides to every story. Even with fortune cookies. Most people take them at face value, but if you ask me, there's always a hidden meaning. You just have to look.

Example #1

Fortune: You are a very kind and patient person.

What it really says: Wake up. Everyone's walking all over you, and you don't even see it.

Example #2

Fortune: Your wisdom will guide you through a difficult situation.

What it really says: You're on your own. Don't even bother asking for help because you won't get any.

Example #3

Fortune: You will soon receive a surprise in the mail.

What it really says: You know that package you just got? Hold it up to your ear. If it's ticking, think twice before you open it.

Angel Desmond

RESIDENT ASSISTANT APPLICATION

In the space provided below, please list five reasons you believe you would be an asset to the RA program.

1. I'm very personable and easy to get along with, so other students would be comfortable talking to me about their problems and concerns.

All right, that's a good one. This is going to be easy.

2. I work well with others and can easily take on leadership roles or sit back and assist while someone else leads.

I'm a shoo-in for this position. How could they not hire me?

3. I'm responsible and trustworthy.

Except for the fact that I just gambled away my entire college fund in one night at the racetrack.

4. I'm a hard worker and a good problem solver. I've held down a job fixing cars at my father's garage ever since I was old enough to lift a screwdriver.

Although he did fire me because of the whole gambling thing.

5. I'm ready to face the challenges of being a good RA, and I believe I could enforce university policies in a fair and effective manner.

Besides, if you don't hire me, I won't be able to afford college at all, so I'd pretty much do anything you asked me to at this point.

Elizabeth Wakefield

Once, when I was in fifth grade, I crossed the road without waiting for my bus driver to wave me on. She made me write "I will not cross the road without waiting for the signal from Lucille" one hundred times as a punishment, and I never forgot to look up at her again. So here goes:

1. I will not think about Conner McDermott.
2. I will not think about Conner McDermott.
3. I will not think about Conner McDermott.

Ugh!

4. I will think about Conner McDermott whenever something Conner related passes in front of my eyes. Like a guitar. Or a Monopoly game. Or a Mustang.
5. I will think about Conner McDermott even when something not remotely Conner related passes in

front of my eyes. Like crab cakes. Or a gum wad. Or a ministapler.

    6. I will mope around thinking about Conner until he begs me to come back.

    I don't need to write that one a hundred times. It's already etched in my brain.

CHAPTER
Moving On
1

"God, Jess. What's in here? Wet towels?" Steven Wakefield asked, groaning as he loaded a large box marked Jessica's Room into the back of his tan Explorer.

Jessica glanced at the crate her brother was carrying and squinted.

"No, I think that's the one I packed with all of the silver from the Fowlers' kitchen," she said, throwing a saccharine smile at Lila Fowler. Steven chuckled, but Lila didn't look amused. She had been hovering around the entrance to her family's mansion all morning, watching Steven, Jessica, and Elizabeth as they packed their belongings into their cars.

"Very funny," Lila said, glaring at Jessica. She took a long sip of ice water from her crystal glass. "Not that I'm totally convinced you're kidding," she added, crossing her arms over her chest and leaning back against the white stucco archway that led into the main foyer. Jessica watched as her sister, Elizabeth, squeezed past Lila with another load. Lila didn't budge.

"Next time I'll go *through* her," Elizabeth muttered to her sister.

"Oh, please, let me," Jessica whispered back. It was bad enough that she'd had to live with the Fowlers the entire time Lila and Melissa Fox were collaborating to make life hell for Jessica, but did Lila really have to be there on the day that the Wakefields were finally moving out?

It doesn't matter, Jessica decided. *We're getting out of here and into our new house. Not even Lila can ruin this day.*

"What are you doing out here anyway?" Jessica asked, running a hand through her fine blond hair as she headed back toward the house. "Don't you have riding lessons or something?"

Lila smiled tightly. "Let's just say I'm making sure that you don't *accidentally* leave with any of my clothes. I know how easy it is to get my designer labels mixed up with—well, whatever it is you wear these days," she said, gesturing at the plastic-wrapped garments Elizabeth was carrying.

Jessica sighed. Lila was such a snob that her comment was almost funny. *Almost.* "As if I'd steal anything from your overpriced, overrated wardrobe," she said, walking back toward the foyer for another load.

"Well, you didn't seem to have any problem with stealing Melissa's boyfriend," Lila said.

Jessica stopped in her tracks and closed her eyes,

determined to keep her cool despite the fact that she could feel her cheeks flaring.

"Come on, Lila. Everyone knows that was a lie," Jessica said. "Why don't you get some new material?"

Lila's eyes widened. "You mean that wasn't true?"

Jessica groaned. "You know it wasn't," she said, clenching her fists at her sides.

"Then what's he doing here?" Lila asked, all innocence.

Jessica's brow furrowed. "What are you . . ."

Her voice trailed off as she followed Lila's gaze. A blue Blazer had just pulled up, and Jessica was fairly certain she knew who was behind the wheel. *Oh God, not now,* she thought, her heart skipping a beat. Will Simmons jumped out of the Blazer and began walking toward her even as she wished him away.

Jessica exchanged a nervous glance with Elizabeth and then focused what she hoped was a bland expression on Will. *Bland equals not interested equals go away,* Jessica thought. She only hoped he would get the hint.

"Hey," Will said, smiling warmly at Jessica. The hint had obviously misfired, and unfortunately Jessica could never keep herself from grinning like an idiot when he smiled at her. "Lila," he said, nodding stiffly in her direction. Lila glared at him and walked inside. Will smirked. "I don't think she likes me."

"Join the club," Jessica said. She sounded normal. Odd, considering the fact that her heart was doing

3

distinctly abnormal dance moves. "I think I'm number one on her most hated list."

"Tell me you left something behind for her," Will said, his eyes sparkling. "You know, like blue dye in her shampoo or shaving cream in her shoes."

Jessica laughed in spite of herself. "Where were you two days ago when I had time to plan something like that?"

"I would have been here." Will shrugged and looked her directly in the eyes. "All you had to do was ask," he said quietly.

Jessica's stomach flopped, and she wrapped her arms around her waist. This was not good. She could not let herself fall for this guy all over again. Not after everything he'd done.

"Um, Will?" she began, narrowing her eyes. "I don't mean to be rude or anything, but . . . what are you doing here?"

Will took a step back. "Oh, I . . . uh . . ." He hesitated. "I wanted to thank you for helping out with the kidnap breakfast earlier. I think it went really well."

Jessica tried not to think about the part that had gone *really* well.

"Like when we picked up Josh," Will continued.

That would be the part, Jessica thought. A shiver passed through her as she remembered the lip lock in Josh Radinsky's bedroom. Lying on the floor with Will's body pressed against hers—*stop*.

4

"What do you mean?" she asked, startled at how panicked her voice sounded.

Will smiled again. "Just that everyone was really having a good time by then. What did you think I meant?" he asked. She could tell he was trying hard not to laugh.

"I better get back to work," she said, her face in full-on blush mode. She gestured toward the house. "We're moving."

"I figured that out already," Will said as Elizabeth walked by him, rolling a hand truck full of boxes in front of her.

Jessica laughed, feeling totally lame. Will gazed at her, the same intense look in his eyes that had been there before they kissed yesterday.

I'm lame, and he's still all over me, Jessica thought. *What am I supposed to do with that?*

"So anyway, thanks for stopping by," she said, staring awkwardly at Will's sneakers. She waited, but he made no sign of leaving. *Why can't I get out of this gracefully?*

"Can I help?" Will asked, leaning down to catch Jessica's eye.

"Oh, um . . ." Jessica shifted her eyes to the sky momentarily and then back to Will. "That's really nice, but you don't have to—"

"Did I hear someone offer to help?" Steven interrupted, extending his hand to Will. "I'm Steven, Jessica's brother," he said, smiling.

"Will Simmons," Will replied, shaking Steven's hand.

"Good to meet you," Steven said. He snuck a glance at Jessica and raised his eyebrows.

Oh, great, Jessica thought, closing her eyes. She could see the wheels spinning in Steven's mind as he decided that Will must be Jessica's new boyfriend. Now she was in for hours of really uncreative mocking at her brother's hands.

"Anyway," Jessica said. "Will was just saying that he has to get going. He just stopped by to—"

"Help," Will finished, nodding at Steven. "But it looks like I'm a little late," he added, gesturing at the Explorer.

"Don't worry," Stephen responded with a laugh. "There's more inside. Jessica alone must have packed twenty boxes."

All right, that's enough, Jessica thought, turning to face Will. "You know, it's really nice of you to offer, but the truck's almost full, so it really doesn't make sense for you to—"

"Good point," Will said, his index finger and thumb extended like a gun for emphasis.

Oh, just shoot me and get it over with, Jessica thought.

"I'll back up the Blazer and we can start filling that," he suggested, looking at Steven for approval.

"Great," Steven said. "I sent Liz for some rope, but I don't know where she went."

"I've got some in the back of the Blazer," Will offered.

"What are you, a Boy Scout?" Jessica said.

"Always be prepared," Will answered with a grin.

"Good. Why don't you get that and I'll grab my keys?" Steven didn't bother to wait for an answer. He just ran into the house, leaving Will and Jessica alone on the front lawn.

"Will," Jessica said, taking a deep breath and looking into his eyes. "What are you doing?"

"Helping you move," Will said matter-of-factly.

Jessica sighed. "You know what I mean."

"Look, Jess," Will began, his face becoming serious. "I'm not gonna just let this go. Not this time."

Jessica looked back at him, dumbfounded. "But—," she started. *But what?* she thought. *I don't want you here? It's not right? I like someone else?* She wasn't sure any of those things were true. Part of her *did* want Will here or at least didn't want him to leave.

"It's just that—"

"Here comes your brother," Will interrupted, nodding toward the door. "I better get that rope." And then he jogged off, leaving Jessica staring after him.

"Hey, for once your jock fetish is working in our favor," Steven said, clapping Jessica on the back as he walked by. "Seems like a nice guy," he added, looking over his shoulder.

"Yeah, that's what I thought too," Jessica said quietly to herself. Just then her parents pulled into the driveway, back from opening up the new house. Jessica watched as Steven introduced them to Will and her parents took turns shaking hands with him.

They probably think Will is some clean-cut, good-looking, helpful friend of mine instead of the reason half of Sweet Valley still thinks I'm a slut, Jessica thought. She shifted her weight from one foot to the other and blew a stray strand of hair off her forehead.

"Next they'll be inviting him over for dinner and referring to him as 'that nice boy, Will,'" she muttered.

Jessica squinted and pinched herself hard on the forearm, but when she opened her eyes, they were all still there. *Great,* she thought, wincing. *It's real.*

"So you're okay, then?" Megan asked, her green eyes wide and innocent. *And naive,* Conner thought. *So naive.*

"Yes, honey. I'm fine," Mrs. Sandborn reassured her daughter, brushing back the strawberry-blond bangs that framed Megan's round face. "Just a few bumps and bruises, but nothing serious," she added, smiling despite the bulky bandage covering most of her nose.

Conner cleared his throat. "So, Mom," he began, eyeing his mother from his standard-issue, beige vinyl chair in the corner of the hospital room. "What happened?"

Mrs. Sandborn shook her head gently and waved one hand in the air as if the whole situation were just an unfortunate misunderstanding.

"Oh, it was nothing, really," she said with a tight smile.

Conner leaned forward in his chair, resting his elbows on his knees. *I can't wait to hear this one.* His mother threw him a stern look—almost as if he had spoken the words out loud—then she smiled in Megan's direction and continued.

"I was on my way home from my meeting, and—"

"Actually, Mrs. Lewis dropped you off at home after the meeting," Conner interrupted. "I think you were on your way out again." He glared at his mother with unyielding eyes as he spoke.

Mrs. Sandborn met Conner's gaze with a rigid stare of her own, but then her features softened as she appeared to contemplate his words.

"That's right," she said finally. "I guess the accident must have confused me a bit." She used her hands to lift herself into a more upright position in the silver-framed hospital bed. "I was on my way out for milk," she continued, nodding in Conner's direction as if the memory had just come back to her. Then, turning to Megan, she added, "I wanted to make sure we had plenty for breakfast. I know how you like your cereal in the morning."

Oh, please, Conner thought, exhaling sharply and rolling his eyes, but his mother took no notice.

Instead she reached over and squeezed Megan's arm, which was resting on the side of the bed. She grasped her daughter's hand and held it firmly in her own as she finished her story.

"Anyway, when I came around that blind corner on Maple Avenue, there was a car parked off to the right—a stupid place to park, if you ask me," she added in an almost indignant tone. "And that's when it happened. I didn't have time to think. I slammed on my brakes, but it wasn't enough, and I ended up hitting the car."

"Oh, Mom." Megan winced. "I'm so glad you're all right."

Conner sighed heavily. "Well, I'm just glad no one else was hurt," he said, his voice flat.

Megan glared at him. "Conner—"

"You were drinking, weren't you?" Conner demanded, his accusing eyes turned on his mother. His heart was pounding so hard, he might have been facing his worst enemy instead of his mom. But sometimes that's what his mother seemed to be—an adversary.

"Conner McDermott," his mother spat, her forehead creasing. "Watch your tone, please."

Conner dropped his head as a contemptuous snort escaped through his nostrils. "Mom," he said, raising his eyes to look at his mother again. "We saw you." He looked at Megan, but she was staring at her mother's hand stubbornly. "We *both* saw you." Megan didn't even flinch.

Mrs. Sandborn sighed and shook her head, staring at the ceiling.

"Honestly, Conner," she said. "You say it as if it were a crime."

Conner opened his mouth to inform her that drinking and driving was indeed a crime, but his mother spoke first.

"Since you brought it up, though, yes. I had a few drinks with dinner," Mrs. Sandborn continued reluctantly. "Not that it impaired my judgment, mind you."

Conner hung his head again, focusing on the lines in the linoleum floor, too angry to speak. He alternately clenched and relaxed his jaw, aware that his mother was willing him to look at her, but he wasn't about to oblige. Even Megan was staring out the window now, as if she were wishing herself anywhere but in this hospital room. Conner hated having Megan in the middle of all this tension, but he wasn't the one who had brought them all together like this today. And this time he couldn't shield her from the reality of the situation. This time his mother had gone too far.

"I suppose it's good that you asked," Mrs. Sandborn said softly, breaking the silence. Conner looked up, but his mother was staring straight ahead, as if she were speaking to someone on the television rather than him or his sister. "It just happens that they did a Breathalyzer test on me last night—standard procedure, of course," she assured them. "And I *was* a tiny bit above the legal limit. So it looks like I'll have to go to court."

Conner's chest tightened, and he clasped his hands in front of him, staring at the red-and-white patterns the pressure of his grip made on his skin.

How could you let this happen, Mom? he thought, feeling like all the blood vessels in his head were about to explode.

He glanced over at Megan, who was so pale, she could have blended into the bedsheets. Mrs. Sandborn, on the other hand, was still gazing at the wall and speaking as if her words had no consequence. She might as well have been reciting a grocery list. *Doesn't she have any clue that she just scared her daughter to death?* Conner thought, glaring at his mother.

"Will you have to go to jail?" Megan asked, sounding like she was about four years old.

Mrs. Sandborn laughed and stroked her daughter's hand. "No, honey. Of course not. It's more of a formality than anything else," she reassured Megan. "In fact, I've already talked with Donnie, and he's managed to set up a speedy hearing first thing tomorrow morning."

"Donnie?" Conner asked, narrowing his eyes.

Mrs. Sandborn immediately tensed, then placed one hand on the back of her neck. Her face contorted with pain as she rubbed the base of her skull, but she didn't complain. Keeping up appearances as always. Everything was fine—as always.

"You know Donnie," she said. "He represented me when . . . well . . . during my divorces."

"Oh . . . him." Conner nodded. Megan bowed her head. This wasn't exactly a topic the three of them talked about freely.

"Anyway, he's a good lawyer," Mrs. Sandborn continued. "Which reminds me . . . he thinks you should both be there for the hearing," she said, looking from Conner to Megan and back again. She spoke the words rapidly, as if she were trying to sneak them in.

Conner shook his head and stared at his mother in disbelief. *What the hell is wrong with her?* he thought bitterly. "Why?" he snapped, throwing up his hands. "Why should Sandy and I have to sit there and suffer through *your* humiliation?" Sandy was Conner's nickname for Megan.

"Donnie thinks it will look better to the judge if my family is there to support me. That's all," she said, looking down her nose at him. Her eyes were as sharp as knives. She was actually trying to intimidate him.

It wasn't going to happen. Conner stared back as if his life depended on it.

"Megan, dear," Mrs. Sandborn said quietly, forfeiting

13

the staring contest for a moment to pick up a cup from the bedside table. "Could you do me a favor and fill this with ice water?"

Megan took the plastic cup from her mother's hand and nodded. "Sure. I'll be right back." As she left the room, she threw Conner a threatening glance. Maybe his sister wasn't as naive as he'd thought.

Conner watched Megan leave. When the door closed behind her, he turned to face his mother. "There's no way I'm going to bail you out of this one, so don't expect me to show up tomorrow, playing the loving son." He watched his mother's face flare with anger and felt his own fury growing within him. "You did this, and you're going to have to deal with the consequences for once. We're not going to make it easier on you." He stood up, ready to walk out of the room and close the door on this conversation.

"Oh, really?" Mrs. Sandborn snapped, sitting as erect as possible on her slightly reclined bed. "Do you want me to go to jail?"

Conner's stomach clenched, but he whipped around to face her. "Better than having you come home drunk every night," he spat.

"And just where do you think you and Megan would end up?" Mrs. Sandborn asked. "You're still a minor, you know."

Suddenly Conner felt like an animal caught in a trap. He realized with sickening dread that she was right. The state wouldn't allow him and Megan to live alone, and Conner knew exactly where they'd end up. *In Seattle. With Gary.* There was no way he was going to let that happen.

Conner stared at his mother resentfully, not wanting to give in. But there was nothing he could do. He put his hands on his hips and looked down at his boots.

"Fine," he said to the floor. "I'll go to court." He heard his mother lean back in her bed and began to walk toward the door once again.

"One more thing, Conner," his mother said as he grasped the metal door handle. Her voice was calm and steady, without a trace of the anger it had contained seconds earlier. Conner stopped where he was, waiting for her to finish. "Be sure to dress nicely," she said. "Wear a jacket and tie. We want to make a good impression."

Conner shook his head. "Whatever," he called back over his shoulder, jerking open the door. *Whatever.*

"Where do you want this one?" Will asked, walking into Jessica's new room with yet another brown cardboard box in his arms. Jessica glanced around. Aside from the full-size bed her parents had set up that morning, a few built-in shelves, and the numerous other boxes littering the floor, the ivory room with its pale blue carpet was bare.

"I guess you can just put it on top of the others," Jessica said, gesturing at the far wall, where most of the cartons had been stacked. "Are there any more?"

Will shook his head as he set down the box. "Nope. I think that was the last one."

He was staring at Jessica expectantly, but she was at a loss for words. Nothing new, considering she'd barely spoken to him since he'd arrived. Jessica turned away and walked over to the two large windows that overlooked the front yard. The stone walkway and the newly planted, bright green lawn, which had been the center of activity all afternoon, were now abandoned.

Jessica gazed out at the once familiar neighborhood. Most of the houses had been rebuilt, like hers, with a few minor changes, but some of the lots stood empty, and others were still in the first phases of construction.

"It's weird to be back," she said, almost to herself.

"I bet," Will said, surprising Jessica with his proximity. Goose bumps formed on her arms as Will's hot breath tickled her neck.

"So everything's inside?" Jessica asked, stepping away from the window and Will. She began adjusting the hangers in her closet as if every item needed to be spaced precisely one centimeter apart. "I thought there was another whole truckload out there."

Will shook his head. "Just what was left in your

parents' station wagon," he answered, moving closer once again. He stopped only inches away. "And Steven, your dad, and I took care of that in like five minutes."

"Oh," Jessica said, her voice cracking.

"Are you okay?" Will asked, his eyes riveted on hers.

Jessica cleared her throat and fumbled with the small stone on the choker she was wearing. "Yeah, fine," she answered quickly. She raised her eyebrows and shook her head. "There must be a draft in here or something," she said, trying to laugh casually as she rubbed at her increasingly bumpy arms. Why was he still here?

"Okay, then." Jessica clapped and turned away from the closet abruptly. "I should probably start unpacking, so you really don't have to stick around." She walked over to the stack of boxes, hoping Will would take her up on her suggestion. Maybe if he left, she'd be able to get a handle on her obviously out-of-control emotions.

"I'll help," Will suggested, following her.

Jessica stared at him. Was she that bad at dropping hints, or was he just that stupid?

Trying in vain to ignore Will's presence, Jessica lifted one of the boxes and placed it on her bed. She pulled at the cardboard flaps, but they didn't move. She was beginning to regret how industrious she had been with the packing tape. *Please let this open easily before I have to face him again,* she thought, aware that Will had moved to within inches of her once more. Suddenly the adhesive let go, and Jessica was set off balance just enough to give Will reason to put out his arms and steady her before she fell into him.

"Sorry," Jessica whispered, righting herself and tugging at her white cotton T-shirt.

"No problem," Will said, allowing his hands to slide off her shoulders and down her bare arms before releasing her.

Jessica tingled all over, wondering if he could hear her heart pounding or possibly even detect its movement through her shirt.

She took a step backward, trying to maintain her composure. "Um, why don't you go ahead and unpack that one?" she said, pointing at the box she had just opened. "I'll start another one over here." *Way over here.*

"Sure," Will said.

Jessica grabbed another box and set it on the floor in the center of the room. When she saw that Will was busy unpacking, she sat down on her knees and let out her breath.

What's my problem anyway? she wondered. *Jeremy's the one I want, not Will. So why am I acting like such a freak?* She looked up at Will and saw that he was glancing at her too.

"Hey, this looks familiar," Will said slowly, removing something from the box on Jessica's bed. It was the leather journal he had given her.

Oh God, Jessica thought, standing up and practically lunging at him. "I'll do this one," she said, trying to close the flaps, but it was too late. Will reached in and pulled out a velvet box containing the silver necklace that had also come from him. Next he extracted a folded piece of paper, a note card with bold lettering, and a bright red envelope.

This is so humiliating, Jessica thought, her face hot with embarrassment. She took the journal, the velvet box, and the papers from Will's hands and tossed them all back into the cardboard box.

"That's all stuff that I gave you," Will said. "I wasn't sure if you kept it." He looked at her as if he was waiting for an explanation. Jessica wasn't about to tell him that she would have gotten rid of the gifts, but when she'd found herself hovering over the garbage can, she couldn't bring herself to do it.

She closed the box and slid it under her bed.

"I can unpack later," she said, aware that Will was still smiling at her. "I didn't even realize that stuff was in there. I mean, it's not like I could have left it at the Fowlers' house, you know. Lila would have lost it if there was even the slightest trace of me left in the house." Jessica tried to sound convincing, but she could tell from the look on Will's face that she hadn't succeeded. Seeing all the gifts he had given her had obviously been a small victory for him—a sign that he mattered.

But he doesn't matter, Jessica told herself. *I have to get him out of here. After everything he's done, I can't let him back in.*

"So anyway," Jessica said, edging toward the door, "thanks for all the help today, but I'm pretty beat. I think I'm going to leave all of this for later."

Will moved toward the door too, but instead of saying good-bye, he reached above her head and pushed the door closed.

Jessica looked up at him, boxed in between Will and the door. His hand was pressed just above her head and his arm was almost touching her cheek, but she tried to ignore it.

She could hear her family busy unpacking downstairs, but the sounds were muffled. Jessica and Will were alone. Very much alone.

Will placed his other palm on the door too, so that he had one arm on each side of Jessica's head. Then, with his eyes fixed on hers, he began to lean closer. Jessica breathed in deeply, feeling his mouth against hers before they had even touched. She closed her eyes and parted her lips slightly in anticipation, but at the last minute something inside her protested, and she ducked under Will's arm and backed away.

"Look, Will," she said, flexing her hands at her sides. "It's not going to happen."

Will dropped his arms and looked away, obviously frustrated. "There's just too much between us," she said.

"Jessica—"

"Will." It came out like a bark or something. Like a command to a child.

"Okay," he said, nodding. He still wouldn't make eye contact. "Okay." He opened the door and walked out of Jessica's room. She just stood there for a moment.

"Good," Jessica said to herself. "Okay. This is a good thing." She let out a small sigh, walked over to the window, and watched Will climb into his Blazer and drive away. Only when his car was out of sight did Jessica realize she was holding her hand over her heart.

TIA RAMIREZ

French IV, Ms. Dalton
<u>Le Petit Prince</u>
Antoine de Saint-Exupery

1. *Pourquoi le Petit Prince a-t-il quitté à sa planète?*
Ecrivez en français, s'il vous plaît.

GOOD QUESTION. I DON'T REALLY KNOW WHY THE LITTLE PRINCE LEFT HIS PLANET. AFTER ALL, HE HAD WHAT HE NEEDED TO GET BY THERE, AND HE HAD JUST FOUND THAT ROSE AND FALLEN IN LOVE WITH HER AND EVERYTHING, SO I'M NOT SURE WHAT HE THOUGHT HE WAS LOOKING FOR, BUT IT KIND OF REMINDS ME OF ANGEL.

I MEAN, I KNOW WHY HE'S GOING TO COLLEGE, AND I KNOW THAT EDUCATION IS IMPORTANT AND STUFF, AND I DEFINITELY

DON'T WANT HIM TO BLOW HIS WHOLE FUTURE JUST TO STAY HERE AND HANG OUT WITH ME. BUT STILL, I FEEL KIND OF LIKE THE ROSE THAT THE LITTLE PRINCE LEFT BEHIND. IT'S LIKE, HE LOVES ME, BUT I'M NOT ENOUGH FOR HIM. NOT THAT I THINK I SHOULD BE OR ANYTHING. I MEAN, I'M NOT ONE OF THOSE JEALOUS GIRLFRIENDS WHO WON'T LET HER BOYFRIEND GO ANYWHERE OR DO ANYTHING BECAUSE SHE'S SCARED OF LOSING HIM OR SOMETHING. THAT'S NOT ME AT ALL. I GUESS I'M JUST KIND OF . . . I DON'T KNOW. I JUST DON'T WANT HIM TO LEAVE. WELL, I <u>DO,</u> BUT I DON'T, YOU KNOW?

OOPS. I GUESS I'M GETTING A LITTLE OFF THE TOPIC HERE. AND I THINK I'M SUPPOSED TO BE WRITING IN FRENCH.

OKAY. SO WHY DID THE LITTLE
PRINCE LEAVE HIS PLANET?
   LE PETIT PRINCE IL A QUITTÉ À
SA PLANÈTE PARCE QUE . . .
THERE'S MORE TO LIFE THAN
ROSES.

Justice 2 for All

Conner pulled at the bottom of his blue suit jacket and sat down heavily on the hard wooden bench.

"I can't believe this," he muttered under his breath, eyeing the buttons, which formed a neat row at each cuff.

"Conner," Megan whispered, chastising her brother with a sideways glance. "Will you please sit still? You're making me nervous."

Conner looked over at his sister. His *little* sister. She seemed so grown-up in her cream-colored sheath and matching jacket—a big change from the blue jeans and button-downs she typically wore. And with her strawberry-blond hair pulled back in a low pony-tail, he could easily have mistaken her for a college graduate on her way to her first job interview instead of a high-school sophomore.

"I can't help it. This is driving me insane," he grumbled, tugging at the knot of his tie. He unbut-toned the top button of his shirt and rubbed at the bare skin under his bleached and starched white collar. His itchy antics elicited a grin from Megan,

25

giving a little color to her pale, tense face.

"What?" Conner demanded, easing Megan's grin into a giggle. He wasn't in a joking mood, but if he could somehow manage to cheer her up— even into nervous laughter—he'd do whatever it took. "You're just lucky that women's clothing is more comfortable."

"Oh, yeah, right," Megan scoffed. "When we get home, you can try on a pair of tights and some heels, and then we'll talk."

"I don't think so," Conner said. "But you might get Andy to try it." Megan laughed out loud, and Mrs. Sandborn turned around in her seat at the defendant's table, glaring at both of them. She opened her mouth to speak, but she was interrupted before she could reprimand them.

"All rise!" a booming voice called from the front of the courtroom. Conner stood up just in time to see an older woman in a long black robe enter the room. Her gray-white hair was pulled back into a thick bun at her neck, and she wore small half glasses that made her whole face look pinched.

"Court is now in session," the bailiff continued. "The Honorable Judge Janet Carey presiding." The judge took her seat at the wooden bench at the front of the room. Conner's heart was almost the only thing he could hear.

"Be seated," she said, banging her gavel once and thumbing through the papers in front of her.

Everyone sat down. Donnie whispered something to Mrs. Sandborn, and she sat up a little straighter. Conner fought to keep from groaning out loud. He couldn't watch her anymore, so he shifted his attention to the judge.

Her desk and the witness box were stained a deep cherry to match the paneled walls and the pews that populated the back half of the courtroom. The uniformed bailiff stood directly in front of Judge Carey. He appeared to be about six feet tall, but still he was dwarfed by the bench behind him, which sat on a platform at least three feet above the red-carpeted floor. This allowed Judge Carey to look down on the rest of the courtroom as if she were presiding over a group of unruly children.

Justice from above, Conner thought, taking a deep breath. *Let's hope Mom gets some.* He was hoping for enough to knock some sense into her without simultaneously banishing him and his sister to Seattle. *No jail time, just a humiliating punishment—like a suspended license and two million hours of community service,* Conner hoped, feeling more as if he were rolling dice at a craps table in Vegas than sitting in court.

"All right, bailiff," the judge said, tapping her pile of notes on the top of her desk to neaten them. "I'm ready for the first case."

"Docket thirty-two, *State of California versus Eleanor Sandborn.* The charge is driving while intoxicated."

Megan gripped Conner's hand, causing a painful pang in his chest. Her palm felt cold and clammy against his. Judge Carey pushed her glasses down on her nose and watched expectantly as Donnie nudged Mrs. Sandborn and they both stood.

"Counselor," the judge said, acknowledging Donnie briefly before addressing Conner's mother. "How does the defendant plead?"

Donnie turned to Mrs. Sandborn, who looked nervously at him and then up at the judge. "Guilty," she said quietly, in a pious voice that almost made Conner drop his jaw.

This is priceless, he thought, watching as his mother gazed timidly back and forth between her lawyer and Judge Carey. *I wonder how long they rehearsed that.*

"Ms. Sandborn," the judge began in a somber voice. "Do you understand the seriousness of this charge?"

"Yes, ma'am. I do," Mrs. Sandborn replied, nodding for emphasis.

"It says here this is your first offense," the judge continued, examining a sheet of paper. "Tell me, have you ever driven under the influence of alcohol before?"

"No, ma'am. Never," Conner's mother answered. Her voice was so convincing, Conner might have believed her if he hadn't seen her stagger through the front door of their house and up to her bedroom so many times.

Judge Carey leaned forward and squinted. "Do you drink often?" she inquired.

"I wouldn't say *often*," Mrs. Sandborn replied, tilting her head as if to consider the matter. "Maybe once a week?"

"I see. And when you consume alcohol, how many drinks do you typically have?" asked the judge, not taking her eyes off Mrs. Sandborn for a second.

Conner's mother fumbled with the pearls she was wearing and cleared her throat. "Never more than one or two," she lied.

More like nine or ten, Conner thought. Part of him wanted to stand up and yell at her—just tell the judge his mother was lying. His grip on Megan's hand tightened, and he shifted in his seat. It looked like he didn't need to say anything anyway. The judge didn't seem to be buying Mrs. Sandborn's act.

I can't go live with Gary, Conner thought, his conflicted sides arguing against each other. *And I can't live like this anymore either.*

"I see," Judge Carey said, narrowing her eyes. "And do you have any idea of the effect your drinking has on your children?"

Now it was Megan's grip that clenched.

Mrs. Sandborn dropped her head and took a deep breath before facing the judge.

"I would never do anything to harm or even upset my children," she said, her voice quivering slightly as she spoke. "You have to believe me. It kills me that they even have to be here today to witness this hearing," she said, turning slightly toward Conner and Megan. "I'd shelter them from this whole ordeal if I could, but they insisted on coming to support me."

Conner clenched his jaw, both sickened by the way his mother was using him and his sister and worried that it wouldn't work. Judge Carey looked past Mrs. Sandborn to where Conner and Megan were sitting. She adjusted her glasses, stared at both of them, and then began sifting through the papers on her desk again.

She doesn't believe it, Conner thought, his heart beginning to pound in his chest. *I saw it in her eyes. She's going to send Mom to jail.* He felt himself tensing up, all the while trying to appear relaxed so that Megan wouldn't notice. A wave of nausea settled over him as he racked his brain for some way to fix this whole mess.

"Excuse me, Your Honor?" It was Donnie.

Do something, Conner thought, his eyes boring into the lawyer's back. *Anything. Just don't let her send Mom to jail.*

Judge Carey looked up. "Go ahead, Counselor," she said, setting down the papers.

"I would just like to emphasize that this is my client's first offense and that she has been a responsible member of her community for several years now," he said. "She not only sits on the boards of numerous charitable organizations, but she is a community leader and a loving mother, as you can see from the fact that her two children have come to support her. In light of these circumstances, I would like to request leniency on her behalf."

Nice speech, Conner thought, his face growing increasingly hot with each passing moment. *Too bad it's not true.* He stared at the flag in the corner of the room so intently that its red and white stripes began to blur. He was hyperaware of the lake of sweat between his and Megan's palms.

"Is that all?" Judge Carey asked, her voice flat.

"Yes, Your Honor," Donnie answered, nodding politely and leaning to sit down. Mrs. Sandborn smoothed the skirt of her long, white dress underneath herself and took a seat as well.

"Actually, you can remain standing," Judge Carey said before either of them had fully settled in. "I'm ready to rule."

Mrs. Sandborn looked nervously at her lawyer, but he smiled back at her. He seemed to think the quick judgment was a good sign, but Conner wasn't so sure.

Judge Carey leaned forward as far as her wide desk would allow and looked directly at Mrs. Sandborn.

"You speak very well," she said, and Mrs. Sandborn smiled sideways at her lawyer. "Unfortunately, I don't believe a word you've said here today—except 'guilty,' that is." The smile vanished from Mrs. Sandborn's face. "In my experience," the judge continued, "the first DWI offense is rarely the last, and a majority of the offenders have a pattern of alcoholic behavior."

Conner's heart sped up as he listened for the verdict. He tried to swallow, but his mouth and throat had gone dry.

"It is for this reason that I am fining you in the amount of twenty-five hundred dollars, suspending your license for a period of one year, and ordering you to seek immediate rehabilitation."

Megan squeezed Conner's hand hard. He could feel the tension emanating from her rigid body, but he was too busy watching his mother to offer any consolation yet.

"But you can't—," Mrs. Sandborn began, her old, brassy voice finally replacing the polite, timid one.

"I can, and I did," the judge said, her voice stern. "You can see one of our counselors for a listing of acceptable clinics, and your lawyer can explain the details to you."

Mrs. Sandborn opened her mouth to protest, but Judge Carey banged the gavel and began rustling through her papers again.

"Bailiff, next case, please," she said as Donnie took Mrs. Sandborn's arm and gently began to lead her out of the courtroom.

Conner let out his breath as he and Megan stood

and made their way to the aisle, falling in behind Donnie and their mother.

"I can't believe this," Mrs. Sandborn mumbled as they shuffled out of the courtroom. She was obviously shocked. *And maybe she's even a little ashamed*, Conner thought, observing her stooped posture and hanging head. *Finally.*

"Does this look okay?" Jessica asked, stretching the elastic at the bottom of her sports bra and letting it snap back against her chest.

"What am I? The fashion police?" Tia asked, dropping her arms to her side, palms out. She was wearing black wind pants with white stripes on the side and a faded gray T-shirt that had The Girl Next Door printed in peeling navy blue letters across the chest. A few holes around the collar and in the back showed glimpses of the black leotard she was wearing underneath. "This isn't exactly what I'd call a hip outfit." She giggled, pulling her wavy brown hair into a high ponytail.

"I'm not looking for tips from *Vogue* here, Tia," Jessica said. She shut her locker door and stepped back just enough to examine herself sideways in the large locker-room mirror again. "I just want to make sure I don't look . . . you know, *slutty.*"

Tia clicked her tongue. "Jess," she said, angling her chin down and staring at her friend somberly. "You have *got* to get over this."

"What?" Jessica snapped back defensively.

"This whole slut thing," Tia answered, her hands on her hips. "It's old news. No one believes those rumors anymore. Will told them what was up."

Jessica looked up at the ceiling, trying to ignore the tingling sensations Will's name had sent up her spine. "I know, but—"

"Besides," Tia continued, sitting down on the bench between the rows of lockers and pulling on her sneakers, "people have moved on. I think the hot topic of the week is some kind of organized protest against the cafeteria food. The freshmen want to stage a walkout or something."

"Really?" Jessica asked, crinkling her nose.

Tia laughed as she finished tying her laces and stood up.

"I don't know." She shrugged, smiling. "The point is, it's not *you* anymore, so relax."

Jessica grinned in spite of herself. "Yeah. I guess I'm still a little hypersensitive about the whole thing," she admitted. "It's just that . . ." Her voice trailed off when she noticed Melissa and Lila standing by the mirror, fixing their hair.

The moment they saw Jessica looking at them, they turned to face her.

"I heard you moved yesterday," Melissa said, her voice as cold and flat as her blue eyes. "How did that go? Did you have enough help?" She widened her eyes, obviously trying for a look of concern.

34

"Plenty, thank you," Jessica answered in a level tone. If there was one thing she had learned in her dealings with Melissa, it was to keep calm.

Melissa nodded. "I heard Will stopped by to give you a hand," she said.

I haven't done anything wrong, Jessica reminded herself. *And I'm not going to let her get to me.*

"Gee, I wonder who told you that," Tia said, glancing at Lila. She leaned forward and touched Melissa's arm as if they were close friends. "I'd watch her," Tia warned. "She's been known to turn on her friends. Even her best friends." Tia stage-whispered the words so that everyone could hear. Jessica felt her breath catch in her throat. If Melissa's presence hadn't made her feel like a mouse in a den of lions, she might have laughed out loud.

Melissa stiffened, and the smug curl of her mouth went flat. "Let's go, Li," she said, brushing against Jessica as she walked by. Jessica held her ground and stared straight ahead, refusing to meet the spiteful glare she knew Lila was giving her as she followed Melissa down the row and out the back door of the locker room.

Jessica let out a breath she hadn't realized she was holding. It was a good thing she'd gotten Will out of her house before anything happened yesterday. The last thing she wanted was to have Melissa go ballistic again. Jessica was tired of always looking over her shoulder.

She placed her hand on her forehead and turned to Tia. "I used to be a pro at that," she said.

"What do you mean?" Tia asked, shoving her jeans into her locker and shutting the door.

"You know, comebacks—shutting people down," Jessica said.

Tia laughed. "Well, it's a gift," she said, starting out of the locker room.

"Seriously," Jessica agreed, walking behind her friend. "Lila and I used to spend hours hurling insults at each other, but now . . ." Jessica sighed. "It's all because of Melissa, you know. She just makes me so nervous for some reason. I swear the girl is evil."

"You may be right there," Tia agreed.

"What do you think she'd do if she knew Will gave me all that stuff and asked me out and everything?"

"I don't know, but I'd like to see the look on her face. From a safe distance." Tia laughed, heading for the door.

Jessica started to follow but paused when she realized her hands were shaking. "Get a grip, Jess," she muttered. Everything would be fine . . . as long as she continued to keep *Will* at a safe distance.

"Conner? What are you doing?" Mrs. Sandborn asked as Conner pulled out his keys and unlocked the driver's-side door of her red Mercedes.

"Getting in the car," Conner said slowly. It seemed pretty obvious to him.

She came to a stop next to him and placed her hand firmly on her hip. "Well, you're on the wrong side," she said, glaring. Conner glanced over at Megan, who was standing by the rear passenger door, her head bowed.

"Uh, I don't think so, Mom," Conner said, turning back to his mother. "Not if I plan to drive."

Mrs. Sandborn exhaled sharply, blowing a curl of blond hair off her forehead. "Don't be ridiculous," she said. "It's my car. I'm driving."

Again Conner looked over at Megan, whose eyes were now pleading. He tried to stay calm, but after sitting through that trial and listening to his mother complain about the ruling for the last hour, his patience was wearing thin. *Why does she always have to pull this crap in front of Sandy?* he thought.

Taking a deep breath, he faced his mother. "You can't drive," he said calmly. "Your license was just suspended."

Mrs. Sandborn opened her mouth and shifted her weight indignantly from one foot to the other. "First I have to be condescended to by that judge and now my own son? Who do you think . . ."

Conner looked past her at the large white columns of the courthouse and shook his head while she talked. He ignored most of it, trying to let it roll off his back, but when she stepped between him and the car and tried to open the door, he leaned against it with all his weight.

"Conner!" Mrs. Sandborn yelled. "Move your arm this instant! I am your mother, and I won't be driven around like there's something wrong with me!"

"That's funny," Conner snapped, "because I've been carting you around for months. Or don't you even remember that I picked you up every time you got chucked out of the country club for drinking too much?"

Mrs. Sandborn's eyes burned with contempt as she stared at her son, but Conner was pretty sure the scorn in his eyes could outlast hers any day. She glanced briefly at Megan and then stalked over to the passenger side, doing a perfect imitation of a two-year-old.

Conner set his jaw forward, tightening and relaxing the muscles in his face and his fists as he looked at the columns again for some sort of answer, but nothing came to him. Reluctantly he swung open the heavy car door and pressed the button to unlock the others for his mother and Megan. No one spoke as they all slid into the brown leather seats, closing their doors in unison. And as Conner placed the key in the ignition and revved the engine, he was well aware that the only voices he would hear all the way home would be the ones on the radio.

Elizabeth Wakefield

Homeroom: Conner's in Ms. Dalton's, and he never gets there before the bell, so there's not much I can do about that.

1st Period: Walk slowly from homeroom, then get a drink from the fountain outside Mr. Crowley's room. Conner will have to go right past me to get to his history class, so even if I don't see him, he's bound to see me.

2nd Period: He has calc and I have physics, so my only hope is to sprint out of Mr. Ford's room and catch him on his way out of class because after that point we're headed in totally different directions.

3rd Period: If I double back downstairs through the sophomore wing and back up the stairs on the other side, I might catch him on his way to gym class.

4th Period: Awesome—we're both in Mr. Collins's English class.

5th Period: Try to bump into him coming out of Mr. Fallons's room and walk casually next to him (or at least nearby) until the stairwell.

6th Period: Lunch. Sit with Tia and Andy but try to let him get there first so he can't avoid me.

7th Period: Easy. Creative writing. Just try not to act too thrilled to be in the same room with him.

8th Period: Physics and French. Well,

We have to go in the same direction for a while, so as long as he doesn't run, we should be walking together. Or at least in close proximity.

<u>After School</u>: Make an excuse to hang out near Andy's locker, which is in close proximity to Conner's. I'm bound to bump into him sooner or later.

Senior Poll Category #4:
Most Likely to Succeed

Ken Matthews—Maria Slater and Evan Plummer

Elizabeth Wakefield—Maria Slater and Conner McDermott

Conner McDermott—At what?

Maria Slater—Elizabeth Wakefield and Evan Plummer

TIA RAMIREZ—ELIZABETH WAKEFIELD AND EVAN PLUMMER

Jessica Wakefield—Elizabeth Wakefield and Will Simmons

Will Simmons—Jessica Wakefield and Evan Plummer

melissa Fox: melissa Fox and Will Simmons

Andy Marsden—Madonna

CHAPTER

CONGRATULATIONS?

3

"So what are you up to now?" Jessica asked as she and Tia walked off the football field after practice. The hopeful look in her eyes wasn't lost on Tia.

I hate this part, Tia thought. Every time she talked about Angel in front of Jessica or Elizabeth, she actually felt guilty, considering all the boyfriend trauma her two friends had been through lately. She didn't want to flaunt her perfect relationship.

"Nothing really." She hesitated. "Just hanging out with Angel for a while. He's picking me up."

"Oh," Jessica said, staring ahead as they walked toward the redbrick school building. "That sounds cool."

Total disappointment, poorly masked. Sometimes it sucked being the only one with a steady boyfriend. Not that she would ever give him up.

"Do you need a ride or anything?" Tia asked, trying to make Jessica feel welcome.

"No, thanks," Jessica said, pushing her hair behind her ear. "I've got the Jeep."

"That's cool," Tia said. "It must be nice to have

your own car. I mean, I know you and Liz share it, but at least you guys don't always have to bum rides from your friends."

"Yeah, but I think I'd rather have a driver," Jessica said, a sudden spark in her eyes. She pointed across the parking lot.

An automatic grin crept onto Tia's face when she spotted Angel. He was standing next to his car, holding the passenger door for her. Tia adjusted her bag on her shoulder and ran ahead, dropping everything a few feet in front of the car and jumping into Angel's arms.

"Hey, baby," Angel said, laughing as he kissed her. "Do you greet all chauffeurs this way?"

Tia giggled and let her feet drop to the ground, her arms still hanging on to Angel's neck. "Only the sexy ones," she said, staring up at him. She heard Jessica laughing as she caught up to them.

"Hey, Tia, I don't suppose your chauffeur has a brother, does he?" she joked.

Tia patted Angel's firm chest and turned to her friend.

"Sorry. He's one of a kind. But give him a month or two, and maybe he can introduce you to some college guys, right, Angel?" she finished, kissing his cheek.

"I'd say it's more probably than maybe," Angel said, grinning.

"Oh my God!" Tia squealed. "You got an interview, didn't you?"

Angel nodded proudly. "Was there ever any doubt?" he said. But Tia knew Angel had been nervous. She knew he was bursting inside.

"I'm so proud of you," she said, reaching up to hug him tightly.

"Congratulations," Jessica said, smiling. "I'm sure you'll nail it."

Angel chuckled. "Well, I don't know about that," he said. "But I'll find out soon enough. My interview is Wednesday morning. I have to be up there by nine."

Tia felt her heart take a sudden nosedive, and she stepped back. "Wow. Isn't that kind of short notice?"

Angel shrugged. "Not really," he said. "They have to move fast if they want to get their staff together before the semester starts." His focus shifted away from her and settled on his car.

"What are you not telling me?" Tia asked, narrowing her eyes.

Angel looked uncomfortable. His eyes darted around looking at the road, the field, the school, Jessica—everything but Tia.

"Angel?" she asked, her stomach beginning to flutter.

Finally he met her gaze. "It's just that if I get the position, I'd have to leave a little earlier. For training and stuff."

Tia watched him shift his weight from one foot to the other. She was sure she didn't want to know, but she had to ask. "How much earlier?"

Angel glanced over Tia's shoulder at Jessica again. "Why don't we just talk about this later?" he suggested.

"No, tell me now," Tia responded, her voice quiet but firm.

Angel cleared his throat and looked deep into her eyes. "Friday," he said, sounding like a doctor breaking bad news to a patient.

Tia's heart jumped into her throat. "Leave Friday?" she asked. "For the semester?"

This can't be happening. I must have heard him wrong. But from the caged look on his face, she knew she had it right. He was leaving in four days. Out of the corner of her eye she saw Jessica fidgeting with her keys.

"I should probably get going," Jessica said. Tia looked at Jessica and nodded almost imperceptibly.

"Congratulations on the interview, Angel," Jessica said. "I'll talk to you later, Tee." She turned and slowly walked across the parking lot toward the Jeep.

Tia cleared her throat, aware that Angel was watching her closely. *I've got to pull it together. I should be happy for him,* she told herself.

"You okay, baby?" Angel asked, leaning in closer and studying her face.

Tia forced herself to smile. "Of course I am," she assured him. "I'm psyched for you. I knew you'd get an interview."

Angel was quiet for a moment as he looked into her eyes. "But . . . ," he prompted.

Tia sighed heavily. "Okay. I was a little thrown by the leaving-Friday thing. It's just so . . . soon."

Angel wrapped his arms around her and pulled her close. "It *is* soon," he said, hugging her tightly. "But we still have a few days, and we don't even know if I'm going to get the position yet."

Tia hoped for an instant that maybe he wouldn't get the job. But she couldn't think like that. She was disgusted that she even let the thought enter her mind.

She flashed Angel a grin. "Of course you're going to get it," she said, straightening his shirt collar and patting his shoulders, then stepping back to give him a proud once-over. "And I'm *not* biased. You just happen to be perfect."

Angel smiled as he grabbed Tia's duffel and pom-poms and threw them in the backseat. "Oh, yeah, no bias there," he said with a laugh, ushering Tia into the passenger seat and closing her door for her.

Tia watched him jog around the front of the car. *Friday,* she thought, feeling sick to her stomach. *Only four days left. What am I going to do when he's gone?*

And suddenly it occurred to her. She was about to find out what it was like to be one of those girls without a steady boyfriend.

* * *

"I'm glad you guys waited for me," Jessica said, taking a bite of a giant chocolate-chip cookie. "I wasn't looking forward to hanging around at home all afternoon." She, Andy, and Elizabeth were walking through the food court in the mall, scarfing down gourmet cookies and sodas as they dodged packs of kids.

"It was Mom's idea," Elizabeth said, tossing her cookie wrapper into a trash can. "She wants us to check out some furniture she saw when she and Dad were here on Saturday."

Jessica laughed, glancing at her reflection in a store window. "You realize she just wants us to find bureaus so we can get our clothes off the floor," she said.

"I was going to ask you about that," Andy said, wiping his mouth with the back of his hand. "I saw your room, and it's a little on the messy side. Does this reflect a more deeply seated emotional problem we should know about?"

"You're the one avoiding all the lines in the floor," Jessica said, watching Andy's sneaker-clad feet as he practically hopscotched from black tile to white. "Afraid of breaking your mother's back?"

"It's step on a *crack*, break your mother's back," Andy corrected, sidestepping a power walker. "I just do this to keep occupied when I find myself in boring company."

Jessica glanced at him sideways and smacked his stomach with the back of her hand.

"Ouch!" Andy yelped. "Unkempt *and* vicious," he said, drawing back.

"And hungry too," Jessica added, stuffing the rest of her cookie into her mouth.

"How can you still be hungry after that huge cookie?" Elizabeth asked.

Jessica shrugged. "I don't know," she said. "Once I start eating stuff like that, I can't stop. I guess I don't have any willpower." Andy exchanged a look with Elizabeth. "What?" Jessica demanded.

"Oh, I don't know," Andy said, staring at the skylight above them innocently. "*Will* power? Was that a Freudian slip or what?"

Jessica scowled at her sister, who was staring blankly at a bookstore display. "Liz! You told him?" The last thing she needed was everyone asking her what was going on with her and Will when nothing ever would be going on between her and Will. *Ever.*

"All I said was that Will helped us move yesterday," Elizabeth said, holding up one hand in defense.

"And that's *all* he did," Jessica said, giving Andy a stern look. "So don't make a big deal out of it."

"Okay, okay," Andy said, raising his palms in surrender.

"Why does everyone have to keep bringing him up?" Jessica muttered. "It's not like I asked him to come over."

Andy coughed once. "Yeah, but—"

"But what?" Jessica snapped, stopping in the middle of the crowded hallway. A few steps ahead, Andy turned and looked her up and down, as if he were weighing his next words. Elizabeth just rolled her eyes and looked down the concourse, obviously ready to keep moving.

"Well," Andy began. "I was just wondering. . . ." He glanced at Elizabeth, but she wasn't even looking at him.

"Yeah?" Jessica prompted.

"Why'd you boot Will out last night?" Andy asked, leaning against the chrome railing that lined the wall.

Jessica shot another dirty look at her sister. "'All I said was that Will helped us move,'" she recited in a mocking tone.

Elizabeth sighed. "Okay, so maybe I told him a little more," she admitted. She strolled over and leaned next to Andy. "But now that he mentioned it, why did you make him leave? Mom and Dad wanted to invite him over for dinner on Wednesday to thank him for helping."

Jessica exhaled sharply. "They wanted to what?" she asked incredulously. She didn't know why she was even remotely surprised. Her parents were *so* predictable.

"I think she said, 'Invite Will over for dinner,'" Andy said slowly.

"Thanks for the update," Jessica returned.

"I'm here to help," Andy said seriously, sounding like an overly sympathetic therapist.

"Uh-huh." Jessica turned to Elizabeth. "There's no way Will's coming over for dinner. I'm not getting involved with him, all right?"

"Hey, I'm not the one who wants to invite him over," Elizabeth said, holding her hand against her chest.

Jessica scooted aside to let a harried mother with three ice-cream-cone-toting children pass by. "But you don't exactly seem put out by the idea either," she said, stepping closer to her sister.

Andy made a little hissing noise and backed away as if afraid of getting hit by a wayward punch.

"Jess, even you have to admit that he's been really nice lately," Elizabeth said, tilting her head. "He didn't have to give up his entire Sunday just to help you move, you know."

"So?" Jessica said.

"I wouldn't," Andy interrupted. "I'm only helping you shop today because Liz promised me a cookie."

"Andy!" Elizabeth and Jessica said in unison. Andy took another step back and pretended to lock his mouth and throw away the key.

"So, he only did that because he really likes you," Elizabeth continued. "And what other horrible things has he done lately? Let's see, he gave you all kinds of presents and defended you to the entire school. Yeah, I can see why you're so upset with him."

53

Jessica looked up at the ceiling and shook back her hair. "Sarcasm doesn't suit you," she told her sister.

Elizabeth ignored her. "Oh, and he also planned the whole kidnap breakfast," she continued. "And," she said, pausing for emphasis, "he's definitely helped you to keep your mind off Jeremy. You haven't even mentioned him in days."

Hearing Jeremy's name surprised Jessica. What was really weird was that until Elizabeth mentioned him, Jessica *hadn't* been thinking about him. At least not much.

I'm not sure if that's good or bad, she thought.

"I just don't think dinner's such a good idea." Jessica furrowed her brow. "And why are you pushing so hard to have Will come over?"

Elizabeth lifted one shoulder. "I think he deserves a second chance," she answered. "Most people do," she added quietly.

Jessica and Andy shared a sympathetic look. This was obviously about Elizabeth and Conner now. Dangerous territory if she wanted to keep her sister from acting like a zombie for the rest of the day.

"Okay for me to talk now?" Andy said, finally breaking the silence.

"Since when do you ask?" Jessica demanded.

"Jess, you're so sweet," Andy deadpanned. "Anyway, I was going to suggest that you wait until after the party to make up your mind."

"Party?" Jessica asked.

"Oh, yeah," Elizabeth said, suddenly reentering their world. "I meant to tell you. Aaron Dallas is having a party tomorrow night, and you should go. Will should be there, and it will give you a chance to talk to him—you know—in a social setting."

Jessica gaped at her sister. "Excuse me? You're going to a party on a Tuesday night? Am I on *Candid Camera*?" she asked, eyeing the plants for a hidden microphone and lens.

Elizabeth frowned. "Yeah, what's the big deal?"

"You aren't exactly Miss Social," Jessica said.

"That's not true," Elizabeth protested. "I hung out a lot at the beginning of the year."

"Yeah, but I thought that was a phase," Jessica said with a smirk. "Are you going too?" she asked Andy.

"I'll probably just hang out for a couple of hours, then split."

"You have to go, Jessica," Elizabeth said, pushing herself away from the wall. "If only to witness me being randomly social."

"All right," Jessica said tentatively. It had been a long time since she'd made an appearance at an actual party. But she didn't want her friends to think she was coming out of hiding for a guy. Especially for the guy that forced her into hiding in the first place.

"But I'm not going for Will," she said firmly. "I'm going to hang out with you guys."

"Whatever," Elizabeth said. "Now, let's go check out that furniture and get out of here."

"And the fact that she could think I have a problem!" Mrs. Sandborn ranted as she walked from the living room to the kitchen, picking up the newspaper and rattling it in her hand. Conner leaned farther into the book he was reading at the kitchen table, trying to ignore her latest tirade.

"Can you believe she's making me leave *tomorrow?*" she shouted, throwing the newspaper into a recycling bin and heading back toward the living room. Conner set down his book and rubbed at his temples.

"The sooner you leave, the sooner you'll be back," he droned.

"And the only clinic my insurance will approve is in Minnesota! *Minnesota,* of all places!" Mrs. Sandborn shouted, returning to the kitchen with a pizza box this time. "Who does that judge think she is anyway? I'm not an alcoholic, for God's sake."

"Yeah, right," Conner muttered under his breath.

Instantly his mother was in front of him, her palms resting on the table. "What did you say?" she snapped, her eyes burning into his.

"I said, 'Yeah, right,'" he answered, his voice slow and clear.

Mrs. Sandborn inhaled deeply, her eyes fixed on him. "Don't you dare speak to me that way," she roared.

"Don't deny the fact that you've got a problem," he shot back coolly.

Mrs. Sandborn stood up, never taking her eyes off him. "Let's get something straight here," she snarled. "I am your mother, and if you want to continue to live under this roof, you're going to have to change your attitude." She whirled around and stalked into the living room.

Like I'm the one who needs an attitude adjustment, Conner thought. Still, he knew that fighting with his mother the night before she left was only going to make matters worse. When Mrs. Sandborn returned to the kitchen with an armful of dirty dishes, Conner forced himself to take things down a notch.

"Minnesota's not so bad," he offered. "As long as you're getting help—"

Mrs. Sandborn set the plates down in the sink, and Conner heard her take a deep breath. Slowly she turned to face him, her eyes cold and her jaw fixed.

"I do not need help," she said, her voice clipped and measured. "And I'm not about to let those touchy-feely freaks at the clinic tell me that I do. I'm going because I have to—*not* because I have a problem." With that, she turned and stormed out of the room.

Conner dropped his head back and stared up at the ceiling.

"Please knock some sense into her while she's gone," he said, not having a clue who he thought he was talking to. "I can't take this anymore."

He sighed, feeling like an empty hole was expanding in his stomach, leaving behind nothing but the dull ache of pressure, disappointment—and fear, an emotion Conner refused to acknowledge.

He picked up his book again, but his hands were shaking, causing the pages to tremble ever so slightly—making the words blur.

"I'm outta here," Conner muttered, dropping the hardcover and whipping his jacket off the back of his chair. He had better things to do than worry about a woman who'd never bothered to worry about anyone.

Not him. Not his sister. Not even herself.

Megan Sandborn

I'm not stupid. I know my mom drinks.
Conner tries to hide it from me, but
I've seen her come in loaded before,
and that day Liz and I saw her at the
country club . . . Well, I didn't exactly
think she fainted from fatigue. But she
can't really be an alcoholic, can she?
Alcoholics are fat men in their forties
with a perpetual five o'clock shadow
and breath that reeks of whiskey.
They're guys who beat their wives and
can't speak a complete sentence
without slurring all their words
together. They're the people passed
out on park benches with a newspaper
over their heads and an empty bottle
propped up next to them.

They're not mothers.

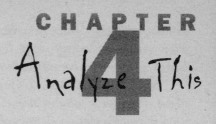

CHAPTER 4
Analyze This

"I can't believe Mom's leaving today," Megan said, slouching in the front seat of Conner's car on their way home from school. It was the only thing she'd said during the entire ride, and Conner knew she was really dreading her mother's departure. He wasn't exactly looking forward to the awkward good-bye scene himself, but he struggled to come up with something encouraging to say to his sister.

"Hey," Conner said, making a right turn onto their road. "You've still got me."

Megan stared through the windshield. "Is that supposed to make me feel better?"

"It wasn't supposed to make you feel worse," Conner offered, shrugging. Megan smiled weakly.

At least it was a change of expression.

He made a right turn onto Orchard Avenue and focused on the distant red mailbox that marked their driveway. "You know, it's only a month," he said. "That's what—four soccer games?"

Megan sighed, blowing her bangs off her forehead. "I guess," she said. "Maybe you're right. A month isn't *that* long. Maybe you and Mom will even get along better after some time apart," she added, glancing at him from the corner of her eye.

"Yeah," Conner said, trying to sound genuine. *Good thing we're almost home,* he thought. *We can drop that conversation right here.*

Conner gripped the steering wheel, feeling a small knot in the pit of his stomach but not nearly as much anxiety as he had expected to feel when this moment finally came. In a lot of ways he was actually looking forward to playing up his big-brother role for a while. And without his mother around to screw things up, maybe he and Megan could actually lead a seminormal life for the next thirty days. But as he pulled into the driveway, all semipositive thoughts flew out the window and his heart froze.

"No," Conner murmured, slamming on the brakes. There was a black Lexus with Washington plates parked near the garage door. *Oh God,* Conner thought. *It can't be.*

"Dad!" Megan yelled, leaping from the car and running toward the house. Conner watched as a short burly man, with a ring of brownish red hair around his balding head, stepped out the front door. He scooped Megan up in his arms and gave her a big bear hug, waving in Conner's direction as Megan dropped down to the ground.

Conner closed his eyes and took a deep breath, fidgeting with the keys in the ignition. *He's not staying,*

Conner thought, willing himself to stay calm.

Slowly Conner swung open the heavy metal car door and stepped out, taking his time retrieving both his backpack and Megan's from the backseat. Megan and her father went inside, and Conner walked with a measured pace to the house.

"I told you she'd be thrilled to see you," Conner's mother said just as Conner reached the kitchen doorway. Mrs. Sandborn was sitting at the kitchen table with the newspaper in front of her and a large red suitcase on the floor. Hanging back, Conner glared at Gary, who was leaning against the counter with Megan at his side. Just the sight of his former stepfather made him want to retch.

"Yeah, it was nice of you to stop by," Conner said, pushing through the front door and setting the backpacks down heavily on the red ceramic-tile floor.

"Hey, Conner. How are you doing, man?" Gary asked, extending his arm and flashing a wide grin that exposed coffee-stained teeth beneath a neatly trimmed mustache.

Man? Conner thought, reluctantly shaking Gary's hand. "Fine," he answered, breaking the handshake prematurely.

"I see you've still got that beat-up Mustang. One of these days we'll have to get you into a real car." He nodded toward the window. "Did you see my Lexus?"

"Yeah, it's real . . . slick," Conner said, curling his lip slightly. "So," he continued, glancing up at the clock, "did you come all this way just to see Mom off?"

Gary and Mrs. Sandborn exchanged a look.

"Not exactly," his mother said. "Gary is going to be staying here while I'm gone." Conner's chest tightened, and he felt his blood pressure rising.

"Really?" Megan asked, her voice laden with restraint. Even she knew not to trust everything the guy said, no matter how much she wanted to.

"Mom," Conner said evenly. "We need to talk."

Mrs. Sandborn studied his face. "Of course," she said, following him into the living room.

As soon as they had rounded the corner, Conner turned on her. "You never told me about this," he snapped. "You know that I can take care of Megan."

"Conner, you need someone here—"

"So you asked a guy who ditched us without so much as a good-bye to chaperon us for a month?" Conner demanded, searching his mother's face for some indication that she hadn't gone completely insane.

"It's not like he completely disappeared," Mrs. Sandborn said. "He does call Megan." She paused and touched her forehead with her hand. "Besides, that's not entirely his fault."

Conner stuffed his hands under his arms. "What's that supposed to mean?"

Mrs. Sandborn shook her head and stared at him

soberly. "Nothing," she said. "The point is, you need somebody here. I wasn't about to leave you alone and have the Department of Human Services take me to court for being a negligent parent."

"If they haven't prosecuted you yet, I doubt this little vacation would change their minds," Conner said.

Mrs. Sandborn drew back, her face so flushed with anger, it was almost the same color as her scarlet blouse. She shook her head slowly, her eyes riveted on his, then dropped her chin and began muttering something under her breath. It sounded like she was counting.

"Look, Conner," Mrs. Sandborn said finally, taking a deep breath and rubbing her hand over her forehead. "I can't deal with this right now. Gary is Megan's father, and he's staying here while I'm gone."

"Then I guess I'll be looking for a place to stay," Conner uttered through clenched teeth, but his mother wasn't playing. She threw her hands up into the air and walked back out to the kitchen, leaving Conner in the middle of the living room, looking for something to hit. He tightened his jaw and tipped back his head, listening as Megan babbled on and on about all the things she and her father and Conner could do together.

"I can't believe this," Conner muttered. One mother in rehab who's sure she doesn't need to be there. One sister who's about to have her heart broken. And a month of having Mr. I'm-okay-you're-okay constantly in his face.

Conner flopped down onto the couch and covered his face with his hands. "And the hits just keep on comin'."

"I heard that Todd Wilkins is helping Aaron with the party," Tia said, munching on a corn chip as she flopped down on Elizabeth's bed. She flashed Jessica a mischievous grin. "So, Liz, are you nervous about hanging out with the former love of your life?"

Yeah, right, Jessica thought, leaning against the door frame. *Elizabeth probably doesn't even remember who Todd is, thanks to Conner.* Not that Jessica minded her sister moving on to hotter, infinitely cooler men. Too bad Conner seemed to want to have nothing to do with Elizabeth.

"Why would I be?" Elizabeth asked without turning around. She was kneeling on her blue carpet, transferring clothes from the floor to her new bureau. She was already wearing a plaid nightshirt and sweats. Jessica frowned. Elizabeth was really going hermit if she was wearing her pj's in the middle of the afternoon.

"I don't know." Tia shrugged. "I just thought it might be a little weird. . . . You and Todd, at an old friend's house, music, dancing . . ."

Elizabeth sighed. "I am *not* dancing with Todd,"

she said. "And if you think there's a chance of us getting back together, you're crazy. That whole thing feels like it was aeons ago."

Jessica shot Tia a warning glance. "Drop it," she mouthed, sensing that Elizabeth was about to turn this into yet another cryptic conversation about her relationship with Conner. Or her *lack* of relationship with him.

"I guess that's true," Tia said.

"Besides," Elizabeth said, turning around to face them. "If anyone should be nervous about the party, it's Jess."

"Excuse me?" Jessica asked, narrowing her eyes.

"Because Will's going to be there," Elizabeth said, shrugging and turning back to her bureau.

Jessica's stomach turned. When were they going to let this drop? "So?" she asked.

"Oh, yeah," Tia said, nodding and digging into her bag of chips. "Everyone's going to be watching him to see what he does."

"What he does about what?" Jessica asked, even though she was sure she knew the answer.

"You," Tia said, causing Jessica's stomach turn to twist into a near panic attack. Tia brushed a few stray crumbs off the front of her leopard-print tank top onto the floor. Jessica just stared at the little chip shards, trying to calm her pulse. Everyone *would* be watching them—especially now that Lila had made sure the whole school knew about Will's moving-man maneuver.

Jessica took a deep breath. "I'm sorry, is that supposed to scare me or something?"

"Umm . . . ," Tia said, lifting her gaze to the ceiling as she pretended to think it over. "Yeah! What if he talks to you? What if he asks you to dance? What if he *kisses* you?" she finished, grinning and causing Elizabeth to snort a laugh as she slammed a drawer shut.

"Come on, you guys," Jessica said. "He's not going to do any of those things because I'm not going to let him."

"Whatever, Jess," Tia said with a self-satisfied smile. She leaned back on Elizabeth's pillows and crooked her arm behind her head. "It's obvious he likes you."

Jessica couldn't have wiped the grin off her mouth if she tried. This was so irritating. She laughed, trying to pass her smile off as a sign of how ridiculous Tia was being.

"And it's *really* obvious that you totally want him," Tia said.

"I do *not* want him!" Jessica shouted. She took a step forward, hands on hips. *That was a little louder than I meant it to be,* she thought, biting her lip as Tia's eyes widened. Elizabeth, being out of it as she always was lately, didn't even flinch.

"O-okay," Tia said slowly.

Jessica dropped her head and sighed. "Um . . . can we just change the subject?"

"Sure," Tia said. They both glanced at Elizabeth's back.

"Oblivious," Jessica said with a smile.

"Totally," Tia said, smiling back and obviously relaxing.

"What?" Elizabeth asked.

"Nothing!" Tia and Jessica both said innocently.

"Anyway," Tia began, running her hands through her hair. "Who *else* do you think will be there tonight?"

Out of the corner of her eye Jessica saw Elizabeth stop in midfold. Her sister's radar was primed for a mention of the C-man.

"I don't know," Jessica started. "I'm pretty sure Maria and Ken are going, and Andy said he'd be there, but . . ."

"But what?" Elizabeth asked, turning around.

Obvious much? Jessica thought. Elizabeth was practically salivating.

"Oh, nothing—it's just that Andy made some weird comment about having some *gardening* to do before the party," Tia answered, wrinkling her nose.

"Oh," Elizabeth said.

"Gardening?" Jessica asked, lowering one eyebrow. "I thought Andy had an aversion to all things green."

Tia giggled. "Who knows?" she said, waving a hand. "I just said 'whatever' and let it go. This is Andy we're talking about."

"Anyone else?" Elizabeth asked.

"Anyone else what?" Tia asked, sitting up and turning to face Elizabeth with her legs swinging against the side of the bed.

"Is anyone else going to the party?" Elizabeth said, adjusting her nightshirt.

"Oh." Tia shot a quick look at Jessica. "Well, Angel, of course, but I don't know about anyone else. I haven't talked to Conner since Saturday," she finished, her tone almost apologetic.

Jessica watched her sister's features droop. *I hope I don't ever get that neurotic about a guy,* she thought.

"Hey, Je-ess," Tia said in a singsongy voice.

"What?" Jessica asked.

"I was just thinking." Tia's eyes twinkled. "Oh, never mind—you wouldn't be interested," she said, waving her hand.

"Whatever." Jessica crossed her arms over her stomach.

"It's not about Will," Tia said, pressing her lips together to keep from smiling.

Jessica felt all the blood rushing to her face as she waited for Tia to break down and spill.

It wasn't happening. "All right, I have a feeling I'm going to regret this," Jessica said finally, "but what is it?"

"Well, since you asked," Tia said, "I was just remembering that Will's a pretty good dancer. But you already knew that, didn't you?"

Jessica felt a shiver course through her body as she remembered dancing with Will in his bedroom. As she remembered his hands on her back, his fingers pressing against her skin, the warmth of his breath on her face . . . Tia cracked up laughing, and Jessica knew her memory was written all over her face. If there had been a pillow anywhere in Jessica's grasp, Tia would have been a goner.

"You know what?" Jessica said, opening the door behind her. "I think my French book is calling my name."

"Are you sure it's not Will?" Tia teased as Jessica escaped into the hall. As soon as she was out of Tia's sight, Jessica covered her face with her hands. If this was her reaction when she was just *thinking* about dancing with Will, what was she going to do if he did ask her to dance?

Jessica glanced at her near purple reflection in the hallway mirror. She was going to have to wear a brown bag over her head. Maybe she could start a new trend.

Conner stood rigidly next to Gary, watching as the taxi driver hoisted Mrs. Sandborn's luggage into the trunk of his yellow car.

"Now, don't you worry," Mrs. Sandborn said, cupping Megan's chin in her hand. "This month is going to fly by, and then everything will go back to normal." Megan nodded and hugged her mother.

Let's hope not, Conner thought.

Mrs. Sandborn released Megan from her embrace and smiled at Gary. "You take good care of her," she said, winking. Gary winked back and grinned. Conner was so revolted, he had to look away, but he managed to check the cynicism in his eyes as his mother approached.

"And you take care of yourself too," Mrs. Sandborn said, leaning in to hug him. Conner was so shocked by the gesture, it took him a second to react. He circled his arms around her and awkwardly patted her back.

Desperately he searched his brain, trying to come up with something profound to say—the one phrase that would make a difference to her, make her *want* to get better.

As she began to pull away, Conner fumbled for the words.

"I love you, Mom," he said quietly, unable to think of anything else. His mother drew back and studied his face. Conner knew it had been a long time since anyone in his house had said those words, and they felt completely unnatural. But he almost had her. He could tell by the stricken look on her face. Unfortunately, almost wasn't enough.

"Me too," Mrs. Sandborn said, nodding, then she climbed into the cab. Conner watched, his stomach in his mouth, as the yellow Ford pulled out of the driveway and disappeared.

Gary and Megan turned to go inside. "Are you coming?" Megan called over her shoulder as she walked through the door Gary was holding for her, but Conner didn't answer. He felt numb, unable to shake the feeling that he had somehow failed.

Moderator: Welcome to our Garden Central chat room. Tonight's topic is Planning Your Herb Garden.

Weedkiller: So what time are you guys heading over tonight?

Maria: Andy? Ken? Are you guys in here?

Greenthumb: Around seven. Need a lift?

Weedkiller: Right here, Maria. But the name's not Andy. It's Weedkiller. And yes, Greenthumb, I could use a ride.

Maria: "Weedkiller"? What's with the alias?

Greenthumb:	I can pick you up at your house. What time?
Weedkiller:	Duh. You're not supposed to use your real name in chat rooms. You should log off and log back on as "Poison Ivy" or something.
Greenthumb:	How about you, Maria? Need a ride?
Maria:	Ken? Is that you?
Greenthumb:	Isn't Poison Ivy a *Batman* character?
Moderator:	Are any of you here for the garden chat?
Maria:	Poison Ivy? Thanks a lot, but I don't think so.
Greenthumb:	Yeah, this is me, Maria.
Weedkiller:	We're all here for the garden chat. Is there a problem?

Moderator:	You don't seem to be discussing gardening. If you're not here for the garden chat, I'm going to have to ask you to leave.
Greenthumb:	But we *are* talking about gardening.
Weedkiller:	Yeah, we're going to a garden party.
Moderator:	Very funny.
Maria:	Andy! You said it would be okay to chat in here!
Moderator:	I'm sorry, but if you don't exit on your own, I'm going to have to eject you.
Weedkiller:	Greenthumb! Pick me up at six forty-five!
	[*Weedkiller* has been ejected from the chat room.]

Maria: And you can pick me up after that, Ken!

Greenthumb: Will do. See you guys later.

[*Greenthumb* has been ejected from the chat room.]

Maria: Thanks. Um, Mr. or Ms. Moderator? I just want you to know that this was Weedkiller's idea.

[*Maria* has been ejected from the chat room.]

CHAPTER 5
DON'T FORGET ME

Conner strummed his guitar forcefully to keep up with the notes being hammered into his head. The music blasting through his headphones was so loud, he couldn't tell if he was on key, but he didn't care. The louder the better.

He had reached for the volume knob, ready to crank it up another notch, when a voice in the background caught his attention. He twisted the dial counterclockwise and listened.

"Conner! How long do you plan to keep us waiting?" Gary yelled from the foot of the stairs.

Closing his eyes, Conner took a long, slow breath. It was actually amazing—the physical effect Gary's voice had on him. Throwing himself out the window would have been preferable to answering the guy.

Conner glanced at the clock. It was seven-fifteen. Fifteen minutes past Gary Sandborn's family feast time.

"No, thanks," Conner murmured to himself, removing his headphones and picking a classic blues riff on his six string.

"Hey!" Gary called again. "Dinner's getting cold! If you come to the table, maybe I'll help you tune that thing later!"

Conner's shoulders tensed so abruptly that he almost snapped the neck of his guitar. Where did the guy get off? He probably didn't know a guitar from a kazoo. Conner waited, frozen, listening as Gary's muffled footsteps headed back to the kitchen. There was no way he was sitting down to dinner with Gary. No way in hell.

Of course, this was going to mean a confrontation, but that was fine with Conner. He'd had enough fights with Gary in the past to know how to handle him.

Conner relaxed his fingers one at a time and gently returned his guitar to its stand. Then, stretching his arms above his head, he stared at himself in the small, rectangular mirror over his bureau, watching as the tiny muscles of his jaw flexed in and out.

Mom should be in Minnesota by now, he thought. *I wonder how many doctors she's managed to piss off so far.*

Conner pictured his mother at the rehab center, insisting she didn't have a drinking problem and then asking for a scotch with her dinner. The doctors would spend the next month trying to help her, and she'd spend it blowing them off.

He glanced at his closed bedroom door.

"Maybe for once she's got the right idea," Conner

muttered. Some things were meant to be blown off.

Conner snagged his jacket from the back of his desk chair and stalked down the hall. He was ready to just head for his car without a word to Gary, but when his foot hit the bottom step of the staircase, one word popped into his head and stopped him cold.

Sandy.

Regardless of how he felt about Gary, there was no way Conner could just leave Megan alone with her father. He couldn't let Gary back into Megan's life just so he could leave and crush her all over again.

Conner flung his jacket onto the bench at the bottom of the stairs and made his way to the kitchen. Gary and Megan were already seated, but from the look of their neatly arranged plates, they hadn't touched their food.

Conner walked over to the empty place setting and pulled out a chair.

Gary frowned slightly, then reached to pick up a basket of rolls. "You're twenty minutes late," he said. "What's wrong? Is your clock broken, or is that . . . music that you play seeping into your brain and affecting your sense of time?"

Conner felt his neck beginning to steam under the collar of his blue-and-white-plaid button-down, but even as he locked eyes with Gary, he could see Megan glancing up at him from beneath her bangs.

It was a gesture that made her round, green eyes seem even larger.

"I don't think the music's the problem," he answered, holding Gary's gaze as he sat down. Gary stared back with equal resentment. Conner wasn't about to look away first.

"Hey, did you see what Dad made for us?" Megan asked in a voice slightly higher than her normal pitch. She gestured toward Conner's plate with a fork. "One of your favorites—ribs."

Conner watched Gary for another moment until the older man finally turned back to his food. Only then did Conner glance down at his plate. Normally just the sight of the spicy sauce would have made his mouth water, but at the moment he didn't have much of an appetite. Conner looked at his sister and nodded.

"And I made chocolate cake for dessert," Megan continued hopefully.

Conner raised his eyebrows. "Sounds good, but I'm not that hungry." He pushed his plate forward, eliciting a heavy sigh from Gary's end of the table. Gary set his fork and knife on the corner of his plate with a clunk and folded his hands in front of him.

"You know, Conner," Gary began. "You're going to have to drop this act if we're all going to live peacefully together for the next month."

Conner leaned forward, his green eyes flashing.

"*Act?*" he questioned. And what did he mean, "peace-fully"? *We'll be lucky if we all live. Period.*

"I think you know what I mean," Gary said, nod-ding. Conner stared at him blankly. "This tough-guy attitude," Gary continued. "And your refusal to ac-cept my role here."

Conner snorted, unable to contain his contempt. "Just what is your role here?" he asked, folding his arms across his chest.

"Well, first of all, I'm Megan's father," Gary said. To Conner's irritation, the statement brought a shy smile to his sister's face. "And for the next month I'm your legal guardian. Like it or not, you've been en-trusted to my care." Conner could almost hear the blood rushing through his veins as he listened to Gary. *As if he's even capable of baby-sitting a televi-sion for that long.*

Gary picked up his silverware again and began cutting his meat. "Although I must say, from a psy-chiatrist's perspective, it's easy to see why you're hav-ing so much trouble with this arrangement," he continued. He speared a piece of meat and shoved it into his mouth.

"Let the analysis begin," Conner said, his voice flat. Gary's coppery mustache bobbed up and down as he chewed.

"You should try this coleslaw, Conner," Megan said, jumping in before her father could respond. "It's really good."

Gary wiped the barbecue sauce from his mustache. "You've got a problem with authority figures," he said. Conner's leg muscles were taut as he tapped his heel against the leg of the wooden chair. "Most likely because your father divorced your mom when you were a baby and then disappeared completely when you were only—what? Twelve?"

Conner's jaw locked at the mention of his father.

Gary calmly slathered butter on a roll. "And even when he *was* around, well, he wasn't exactly in the running for father of the year, was he?" he continued.

"My father was twice the man you'll ever be," Conner spat. His hands clenched into tight fists beneath the table.

"Conner." Megan darted her eyes nervously at her father, but he didn't seem to notice.

"Typical," Gary said, laughing lightly as he shook his head.

Conner leaned forward in his seat. "Wait a minute—"

"Look, Conner," Gary said, holding up one hand. "I just think it's clear that you're having a problem with me because you're afraid if you trust anyone or let anyone get close, you'll just end up getting hurt again."

It took total control to keep from laughing. As if Conner cared one iota about getting close to *anyone*— especially Gary. Conner took a deep breath and leaned back in his chair once again.

"Very interesting," Conner said finally. "I guess that's why you're the shrink."

Gary squinted. "Why's that?"

"Well," Conner said, shrugging, "I would have just assumed I didn't like you because you're a pathetic loser who bailed on his family."

Megan dropped her fork and looked slowly from Conner to her father.

In the stillness of the kitchen Gary's breath was audible, as if he were practicing some kind of relaxation technique. Obviously he was either too much of a wuss or too much of a moron to come out with a decent comeback.

Conner rose from the table and retrieved his jacket from the living room.

"What are you doing?" Gary asked, placing both hands flat on the table.

"I have plans," Conner answered, continuing toward the door. "Maybe you should spend some quality time with your daughter," he said. "Since she won't be seeing you again for another couple of years."

"But then the moderator ejected us all," Maria said, laughing as she patted Ken and Andy on their backs. It was a casual gesture, but Jessica couldn't help noticing how uncomfortable Ken looked as he bowed his head and stared at his feet.

Jessica was surprised Ken had even come tonight.

He didn't exactly look like he was ready to handle a crowd. She gazed past his shoulder, scanning the huge open living room, dining area, and kitchen of Aaron's house. There had to be at least fifty people here already—including Will, who had been hanging out with the football crowd near the island in the kitchen and staring at Jessica ever since she arrived.

Jessica locked eyes with Will across the room. Her shoulders tensed, and she immediately looked away. As long as he was looking at her like that, she was not going to be able to relax and enjoy herself. She glanced over again. He was smiling, still talking to one of his buddies, but his eyes were riveted on her. *I guess Ken isn't the only one feeling a little self-conscious tonight,* Jessica told herself as she ran her hands along the waist of her light blue slip dress, suddenly wishing she'd gone with jeans and a T-shirt instead.

Unfortunately, Tia's prediction was also coming true. Half the football team, most of the cheerleading squad, and a good portion of the rest of the crowd had looked from Will to Jessica and back again at least once tonight. The scrutiny was making Jessica's stomach feel like it didn't belong in her body. Maybe it was time to just call it a night.

Tia leaned in close, startling Jessica and almost making her jump. Jessica wasn't just on edge—she was teetering over.

"Hey, you see the way Ken's looking at Maria?" Tia

asked in a whisper. Jessica glanced at Ken. He was acting sort of like an eighth grader with a big crush. He kept laughing at *everything* Maria said—even when she was just commenting on the tanginess of the onion dip.

"Yeah?" Jessica prompted, expecting Tia to spill some juicy gossip that might take her mind off her bull's-eye status.

"Well," Tia confided, grinning, "that's the same way Will looks at you."

Jessica leaned back and scowled at her friend. "Can we *please* not talk about Will?" she muttered, lifting a red plastic cup of ginger ale and cranberry juice to her mouth.

"Okay, but he—"

"I'm serious, Tia," Jessica snapped. She really couldn't take this anymore. Every nerve in her body was frayed, so when she glanced up and saw Will coming straight at her, she almost spit out a shower of liquid.

"Are you okay, Jess?" Angel asked, patting her on the back as she coughed.

"Fine," Jessica rasped. While Angel and the others watched her with concern, Jessica noticed a huge grin forming on Tia's face and knew that she had spotted Will.

"Um, Angel?" Tia said, grabbing his hand. "I think this is our song." She began to pull him toward the center of the living room, where people had started dancing.

Angel cocked his head. "This isn't our song, baby," he protested.

Tia glared at him. "It is now," she said sternly.

"All righty," Angel said, confused. He let her lead him to the impromptu dance floor.

Maria grabbed Andy and Ken by their sleeves. "I think this is our song too," she said.

"*All* of us?" Andy asked.

"I think I can handle you both," Maria said, leading them off. She kicked up one heel, showing off a funky, red, high-heeled sandal. "Wore my dancing shoes."

"Oh, come on, please you guys!" Jessica stage-whispered, her voice still scratchy from the soda in her windpipe. They weren't making it too obvious. "Don't abandon me."

"Sorry, Jess," Maria mouthed with a shrug.

What was with everyone? Why did they all want her to be with Will so badly? Did they all have amnesia? Had they all forgotten everything he'd done? Jessica glanced in Will's direction. Matt Wells had stopped him to chat, but he was still glancing at Jessica every five seconds.

At least Elizabeth was too preoccupied with looking for Conner to notice anything. "Okay, Liz," Jessica said, clutching her sister's hand. "You're not gonna leave me, right?"

"What?" Elizabeth said, looking down at their entwined fingers. "Why would I leave you?"

Suddenly Andy swooped down on them from the direction of the dance floor just as Will broke away from Matt. "You're leaving her because I need a boogying partner," Andy said, grabbing Elizabeth's free hand and tugging her away from Jessica.

"Oh. Okay," Elizabeth said distractedly.

"Wait!" Jessica said, clutching Elizabeth's fingers.

"Ow! Jess!" Elizabeth exclaimed, tearing her hand away. "I'll be right back." Andy put his hands on Elizabeth's slim shoulders from behind and steered her toward the dance floor.

Jessica watched Andy's gold surfer T-shirt disappear into the bouncing throng. For a moment she considered following them, but Will had already seen her seeing him. All around her there were semi-familiar faces, none of which would ever be helpful in a crisis and some of which had already noticed Will's approach. Jessica was trapped.

"It's okay," Jessica told herself, placing her cup on a nearby table and adjusting the spaghetti straps of her dress. "I can handle this."

But as Will closed in, her hands were getting clammy. She realized she was wringing them nervously and tried to find a comfortable place to put them, but everything felt awkward. Her eyes darted around the room. Lila and Cherie Reese were obviously whispering about her, their pathetic attempt at hiding behind their cups a miserable failure. Suddenly Gina Cho pulled Melissa into the room from the backyard, and Jessica saw Melissa's eyes go wide.

Jessica checked the room for possible escape routes. Every doorway seemed packed with people.

"Hey," Will said, flashing his killer grin. Already his voice was causing chills. "You look great tonight." Jessica glanced down at the silver straps on her shoes.

Should she say "thank you" or "go away"?

Jessica looked up past his shoulder. Melissa's eyes were now narrowed, and she and Gina had been joined by Cherie and Lila.

Not again, Jessica thought. She couldn't deal with the glares and stares and whispers and rumors and heart-wrenching attacks. Not again.

"I have to go," Jessica said to an obviously surprised Will.

"What?" he asked quietly. "Jessica, I don't understand—"

Jessica looked over her shoulder. People were actually blatantly watching them. Not a lot of people, but enough. They'd fallen silent, wondering what was going to happen next.

"Understand this, Will," Jessica said, shocking even herself when she was able to look him in his clouded, baffled eyes. "I don't want you, okay? Just leave me alone."

With that, Jessica turned on one very shaky heel and pushed her way through a wall of spectators, leaving the whispers and stares, and a beet red Will Simmons, behind.

*　　*　　*

"You sure we should have left them alone?" Angel asked, his arms hanging around Tia's hips as they swayed slowly to the music.

Tia looked up at him with half a grin. "Angel, honey. No offense . . . but you're a guy." Angel opened his mouth, but Tia quickly covered it with two of her fingers. "I know you're good with cars and sports and all kinds of male bonding, but playing Cupid? That's my department."

"Okay, I bow down to the love goddess," Angel said.

Tia smiled and snuggled in close to him, inhaling the fresh scent of his cologne and smiling contentedly.

"So," Angel said, pulling back abruptly. "What kind of questions do you think they'll ask me tomorrow?"

Tia sighed heavily and stared up at him. "I can see how a romantic moment with your girlfriend would remind you of your RA interview," she jabbed.

"Come on, Tee," Angel said, cocking his head as if he were talking to a child. "You know this thing is weighing on me right now. I need this job if I want to go to college."

"Hey, let's not forget who talked you into the whole thing," Tia said, shaking her freshly curled hair down her back.

"How could I forget?" he asked, touching his fingers lightly to her face. "But I still need your help."

"Okay," Tia said.

Call me crazy, she thought, staring down at the floor. *I was just hoping we could spend one night together without talking about you leaving for school.*

She took a deep breath and lifted her head. "Okay," she said. "How about, 'Name three of your strengths and explain why they would make you a good RA'?"

"Okay," Angel said. "That's kind of like the question they asked me on my application. First of all, I'm easy to talk to, so other students would feel comfortable coming to me with their problems."

Tia grinned. "It also helps that half the time you're lying on your back with your head under a car," she said with a giggle. "It's way easier to spill your guts when you can't see the other person's face. That's why Catholics go to confession, you know."

Angel stopped dancing and scowled at her.

"Okay, okay," Tia said, wrapping her arms around him and giving him a squeeze. "Go on. I'll be quiet."

Angel studied her face for a minute, then started swaying again. "All right," he said. "Second, there's the fact that—as my lovely girlfriend was kind enough to point out—I've held down a job as a mechanic since I was big enough to hold a wrench, which demonstrates that I'm a hard worker. And when I take something on, I really dedicate myself to it."

Tia smiled and shook her head. "You're smooth," she said admiringly. "There's no way you're not getting this job."

"Let's hope the people at Stanford feel the same way," Angel said. "Okay, now for number three." He stared into the air above Tia's head, concentrating on his answer.

Look how excited he is, she thought, observing the light in his dark brown eyes.

"I know," Angel said suddenly, snapping his fingers. "I'm a people person. That's number three." Tia watched his animated face. He was so cute, so smart, so wonderful. How could they possibly turn him down? "I love meeting new people, and I know I'd have a great time planning activities for the other students—social and educational."

"What kind of events would you plan?" Tia asked.

"Well," Angel started, looking down at her seriously. "I'd try to plan a variety—"

"No, Angel," Tia said, giggling as she grabbed his chin between her thumb and forefinger and pulled his head down toward hers. "It's not an interview question. I was just wondering what kind of stuff you'd be doing." Tia kissed him on the nose and released him.

"Oh." Angel chuckled. "I'm not really sure. I think I'm supposed to come up with a few educational ideas, like speakers on date rape and stuff like that, but mostly I just have to help plan things like ice cream breaks in the study lounge and dorm dances and stuff."

"Dances?" Tia asked. For the past few weeks she'd chosen not to think about the fact that Angel's college experience was going to involve a lot more than just textbooks and lecture halls. There would be new friends, new things to do. New people to hang out with, study with . . . dance with.

"Yeah, sure. And I'll probably have to—"

"Angel?" Tia said, looking up at him.

He stopped and stared down at her, his dark eyes wide with concern. "What is it, baby? You look upset."

Tia tilted her head. "Are you going to . . . dance with other girls at college?" *Other girls,* Tia thought, a lump forming in her throat. *College girls. Women.* She knew how insecure she sounded, but she couldn't stop the images running through her mind. Angel was handsome, and he was a good dancer. It would be stupid to think no one was ever going to ask him.

Angel laughed. "Only if they're cute," he joked.

Tia's heart dropped along with her eyelids. She stared down at the floor, trying not to look like a wounded puppy. Angel's brow creased. Bending his knees slightly to bring his head down to her level, he gently lifted her chin in his palms.

Tia took a deep breath, watching Angel's face soften, the small grooves at the corner of his eyes deepening as he smiled at her. "Of course I'm not going to dance with anyone else," he said, smoothing her hair back with his hand. "You're the only one I want to dance with, Tia."

"I'm sorry," she said, sighing heavily. "Can we forget I ever asked you that? I feel like a total idiot."

Angel kissed her forehead and looked lovingly into her dark brown eyes. "You're not," he said. "But yeah, we can forget about it."

Tia leaned into him, holding him closer. She glanced down at her black knit slip dress and matching crocheted shawl. Suddenly her carefree gypsy-girl look seemed so . . . high school. *And he will dance with other girls. Just like I'll probably dance with other guys.*

But that was different. Tia knew that most of the guys she'd be dancing with were ones she'd known since kindergarten. But the girls Angel would meet at college would be new and exciting. Not to mention older. And more experienced.

Tia pulled her head back slightly, feeling the warm flesh of Angel's neck against her cheek as she did. She looked up at his dark face, trying to picture him dancing with another girl, but just the thought of it made her stomach turn. She didn't want to lose him. Yet somehow she felt like part of him was already gone. Tia stood on her tiptoes and trailed light kisses across his chin.

Angel sighed contentedly, obviously forgetting about his RA interview for the moment. His eyes were closed, and there was a sweet smile on his face, but all Tia could think about was the fact that if he got the RA position, he would be leaving in just three days.

She nestled her face back against his chest. *This could be the last time we dance together for a long time,* she realized, wrapping her arms around him tightly. Angel seemed to sense her desire for closeness, and he tightened his hold on her until no gaps remained between them.

Tia felt his breath in her hair and sighed aloud. In his arms was her favorite place to be. She was unable to imagine anything more perfect than dancing this close to Angel, but as she considered how little time they had left, she felt a sudden need to be even closer.

But how could we possibly be any closer than we already are? Tia wondered, nuzzling into his neck. *There's only one thing we haven't shared, and I don't know if we're ready for that yet.*

Just then Angel leaned down and kissed her softly on the lips. He drew back just enough to look solemnly into her eyes, then kissed her cheek and whispered, "I love you, baby. Nothing's ever going to change that, you know."

"I know," Tia whispered, closing her eyes and enjoying the way it felt to have Angel's strong arms wrapped around her. *I wonder if . . . ,* she started, almost afraid to let her mind form the thought.

I wonder if maybe we are *ready.*

Andy Marsden

<u>Why</u> <u>Parties</u> <u>Are</u> <u>Like</u> <u>Geometry</u>

Parties are basically large social gatherings where groups of people hang out in big circles, eating geometrically shaped crackers with little squares of cheese on them.

Most of the girls there are in search of guys who'll give them a straight line, while most of the guys are working on sharpening their angles.

On top of that, whoever's hosting the party is constantly trying to balance Pythagoras's less famous equation, making sure that $(people)^2 + (fun)^2$ does not equal $(accidental\ destruction\ of\ parental\ property)^2$.

Furthermore, love triangles of all sizes and proportions become blatantly apparent when points A, B, and C are all present in the same room.

And above all, everyone at a party is hoping to be viewed from a complimentary angle.

Jessica jumped when the door to Aaron's bedroom opened, half expecting to see Melissa standing there with some kind of deadly weapon.

"There you are," Elizabeth said, closing the door against the loud music and laughter pouring in from the hallway. "I've been looking for you forever."

Glancing at the clock, Jessica sighed and sat down shakily on Aaron's green bedspread. "I've only been in here for half an hour," she said.

"Right," Elizabeth said, plopping down next to Jessica. "And why is that again?"

Jessica could feel her sister studying her profile, but she kept staring straight ahead at Aaron's poster of the Olympic soccer team. She didn't feel like spilling, even to Elizabeth, but there was no point in trying to keep anything from her thinks-she's-a-psychologist twin.

"Because I wanted to leave, but you have the car keys," Jessica said with a small smile. "So I thought I'd just hide instead."

Elizabeth leaned forward, resting her elbows on

her knees so that she could look up into Jessica's face. "This is about Will, right?" Elizabeth asked. "I saw you bolt when he came over to talk to you."

At the mention of Will's name, Jessica's skin started to tingle. She rubbed at her arms. "Everyone was watching us," Jessica said, glancing at Elizabeth's concerned expression. She suddenly let out a short laugh. "Remember when I used to *like* having everyone watch me?"

Laughing, Elizabeth flopped onto her back, causing the bed to squeak loudly. "How could I forget? It was only your way of life from the moment you were born." Jessica lay down too, and Elizabeth turned her head to face her. "Mom once told me you even cried louder than me in the delivery room."

"Shocker," Jessica said with a giggle. For the first time all night she was actually starting to feel relaxed. Thank God that Elizabeth had found her. Jessica should have known her sister would understand.

"So," Elizabeth said, lifting her hands in front of her face and picking at her nails. "I kind of did something, and you're kind of not going to be happy about it . . . at first."

Jessica sat up straight, her heart pounding. She didn't like that cagey tone. Elizabeth only sounded cagey when something big was up. "What?" she asked, glaring down at her sister.

"Well, I figured if I couldn't fix my own boyfriendless situation, maybe I could help you with yours," Elizabeth said, concentrating intently on her thumbnail.

"What did you do?" Jessica demanded, grabbing Elizabeth's hands and pulling her up into a sitting position. Elizabeth's hands felt oddly warm, clasped inside one of her own.

"I asked Will over for dinner."

Jessica had never fainted before, but she was sure this was what it would feel like. Her vision blurred over, first with gray, then with blue. Her head felt like she'd just popped twenty antihistamine tablets—all fuzzy and heavy—and her heart was pounding in her ears. Then suddenly everything cleared. Jessica jumped to her feet.

"You *what!*"

"And he said yes," Elizabeth said calmly, pressing her hands into the mattress and leaning back casually.

"He *what!*"

Hadn't she just told the guy she didn't want him?

"He's coming over tomorrow night. I told him it was Mom and Dad's invite," Elizabeth said.

Jessica pushed her hands into her hair, holding it back from her face as she stared down at her obviously insane twin. Two seconds ago she'd been eternally grateful for Elizabeth's understanding nature. Now she was pretty sure Elizabeth had somehow been given a quickie lobotomy on the dance floor.

"How could you do this to me?" Jessica asked.

"Don't be so dramatic," Elizabeth said with a

shrug. "I *know* you like him. I just figured you probably panicked because everyone was watching you, which is exactly what you just said."

"So you think I'll be better off hanging out with him in front of Mom and Dad?" Jessica almost shouted. She crossed her arms over her chest. "Why can't everyone leave this alone? It's *my* life!"

Elizabeth sat up straight, staring up at Jessica as if *she* were the one who'd just stepped over the line. "Jessica—"

"Disinvite him."

"What?" Elizabeth asked. "Are you in second grade? It's just dinner."

Jessica was about to crawl out of her skin, but she could tell from Elizabeth's expression and body language—chin slightly lifted, shoulders rolled back—that she wasn't going to get anywhere.

"Fine," she said with a sigh. "But after this, I want everyone to leave me alone about Will. I can make my own decisions about who I want to date."

"Fine," Elizabeth said, standing up.

"Fine," Jessica repeated. They stood there for a moment, staring at each other in silence. Jessica waited for her sister to break the postfight standoff, but she wasn't moving.

"Can we go now?" Jessica said finally.

Elizabeth threw her arm over Jessica's shoulders and steered her toward the door. "Yeah. Let's get out of here. We have a big dinner to plan."

Jessica groaned.

Out in the crowded hallway she used her years of mob-maneuvering experience to get herself and Elizabeth to the front door as quickly as possible, making sure to keep from looking anyone directly in the eye. But just when she thought they were home free, she caught a glimpse of Will on the other side of the living room.

All he did was smile and lift his chin, but Jessica knew what he was thinking. He was thinking he'd won. He probably thought she'd put Elizabeth up to asking him. He probably thought she was too nervous or shy or chicken to ask him herself.

Jessica squared her shoulders, turned her back on him, and whipped open the door, letting Elizabeth through first. She made a decision right then and there. When Will came over tomorrow night, she was going to be the picture of composure. *She* was going to be the confident one, leading the conversation and controlling the situation.

She was going to prove to Elizabeth, to Will, and to herself that he didn't affect her. Even if she turned into quivering Jell-O trying.

Tia searched the first floor of the Dallas house, walking quickly from room to room. Angel would be back any second, and she needed to discuss her brainstorm. Where were her friends when she needed them? Had everyone bailed on her? Checking the dance floor, she caught a glimpse of Andy's red hair popping out of the crowd as he did the Marsden Dance—a patented move that basically involved non-stop jumping. She thought about braving the bumping and grinding crowd to get to him but decided she didn't want to risk the personal injury.

Suddenly Tia saw two blond heads out of the corner of her eye. She turned to yell to Jessica and Elizabeth, but they were out the door. She threw up her hands in exasperation. Maria and Ken were nowhere to be found, Jessica and Elizabeth were AWOL, and Andy was untouchable.

Man, she wished Conner were here. But as far as Tia knew, he'd yet to make an appearance. She just hoped everything was going okay at home. Tia knew his mother had left that afternoon, and she hadn't heard from him all day.

Making her way through the kitchen one more time, she checked around for anyone she could talk to before Angel got back. At least the line for the bathroom had been pretty long. Hopefully he was still occupied.

Opting for the backyard, Tia turned into the doorway leading outside and came face to chest with a suede jacket. A very familiar, very beat-up suede jacket.

"Conner!" Tia said, throwing her arms around his neck. "I'm *so* glad you're here," she said. "I really need to talk to someone."

Conner rolled his eyes and looked off to the side. He didn't hug her back.

"Good to see you too," Tia said, releasing him. "Is everything okay?"

Conner moved away from the door, leading her out of the heavy traffic. "What is it, Tee?" he asked gruffly.

"Well, if you're going to have an attitude about it . . . ," Tia said. She started to walk away, but Conner grabbed her arm, forcing her to turn around again and face him.

He took a deep breath and let it out slowly through his nose. Then he slowly released his grip on her. Tia waited for him to decompress.

"Okay, I'm sorry," he said. "What's going on?"

"Well, you know Angel's leaving for school soon, right? Like maybe even as soon as Friday, and I'm really scared that he's just going to . . . I don't know . . . move on or something." Conner sighed heavily, and Tia knew she wasn't going to be able to keep his attention through the long version of the story. "All right, I'll get to the point.

"It's not so much that I think he's going to forget me or anything," she continued, speaking as quickly as she could. "It's just that I don't want to lose him. Not that I think we'll just split up the minute he leaves, but everyone knows that long-distance relationships are really hard to keep going—right?" Tia observed Conner's numbed expression. "Sorry," she said. "I guess short stories aren't my strength."

Conner closed his eyes. "Look, Tia—"

"Wait," Tia begged, holding up her hands. "I really need your advice. Here's the deal." Conner folded his arms across his chest. Tia took a deep breath. "All right. I've been thinking about it, and I'm kind of wondering if . . . well, I sort of think I might be ready. . . ."

This is harder to say than I thought it was going to be, Tia said to herself, gritting her teeth and pressing her fingertips together as she tried to form the words.

"To . . . you know . . ."

Conner groaned and dropped his head into his hands, rubbing his temples vigorously. "Look, Tee, I'm sorry," he said through his palms. "I just can't deal with this right now. Can we talk about it tomorrow?"

"Conner, I—"

But before Tia could finish her sentence, Conner had made his way to the cooler by the patio doors. He rummaged around in the ice, finally pulling out a long brown bottle and snapping off the top with his key ring.

Tia watched, feeling distinctly hollow, as he took a long sip and then walked out into the backyard, disappearing into the darkness.

"Fine," she said with a sigh. "I guess I'm going to have to figure this one out on my own."

*   *   *

Conner cupped his hands and splashed his face with cold water from the faucet. He shouldn't have had that last beer. Maybe then his reflection wouldn't be staring back at him from the bathroom mirror with dark circles under its bloodshot eyes.

"Or maybe I should just drink more often so it won't affect me so much," Conner mumbled, wiping his nose with the back of his hand. He chuckled bitterly and turned away from the mirror. "Then Mom and I could go to Betty Ford together."

Conner scrubbed his face on a white terry-cloth hand towel, glared at his pale reflection one last time, and threw the towel into a blue plastic laundry basket. On his way out through his bedroom he hefted his backpack over his shoulder and grabbed his worn, brown suede jacket, clutching it in his fist.

If he hurried, he could get out of there before the stepdad from hell woke up. But as Conner headed toward the kitchen, he caught a whiff of fresh coffee. He was about to forgo breakfast and just head out the front door, but he stopped when he heard muffled voices coming from the living room.

It was 7:15 A.M. Who was Gary doing coffee with?

Slowly Conner walked through the kitchen, his rubber-soled sneakers quiet on the ceramic tile floor. He peered around the doorjamb into the living room and spotted Megan and Gary sitting on the couch.

Megan was already dressed for school, and Gary

had thrown on chinos and a polo. They were both bent over one of Megan's textbooks, and they looked so cozy, Conner was tempted to shout, "Fire!" just to get them away from each other.

"Oh, see—that's where you got confused," Gary was saying, pointing at the open page. "You were multiplying by the *radius* of the circle. You need to use the *diameter*."

"Duh," Megan said, slapping her head exaggeratedly. "How could I do that? I'm so stupid."

Gary chuckled. "I'm the one who had to read the first six chapters of your book to relearn the difference between a parallelogram and a trapezoid, remember?"

He was helping her with math homework? Conner's jaw clenched as he fought back a disturbing wave of emotion he didn't want to acknowledge. Why hadn't Megan come to him? He always helped her with her homework.

"Thanks for getting up early to do this with me," Megan said. "I couldn't believe I fell asleep on my desk last night."

"You had a geometric proof imprinted on your forehead when I found you," Gary said with an irritating laugh. He checked his watch. "We'd better get on with this, or you're going to be late."

"Good point," Megan said. "So what about this one? I become brain dead when I look at word problems."

"Let's see." Leaning over the book, Gary started to read the problem aloud, taking quick notes on a pad as he spoke.

Conner's skin was itching with irritation and suspicion. What was in this for Gary? There had to be an angle. Just like there was an angle when he'd married Conner's mother. Just like there was an angle when he'd left.

Standing there in the doorway, spying on his sister like some jealous child, Conner decided it was time to take action. He didn't know what Gary was trying to do, but one thing was certain—there was no way Conner was going to let this loser take his place. He was the one who'd always been there for Megan. He was the one who always would be.

"Hey, Sandy," Conner said, leaning against the doorjamb.

"Hey, Mac," Megan said, looking up with a smile.

"Conner," Gary said.

Conner ignored him. "Want to swing by McDonald's before school?" he asked.

"Seriously?" Megan said, her eyebrows arching.

"We have time," Conner said. "We can finish your homework there."

Megan slammed her book shut and shoved it into her bag. "You don't have to ask me twice," she said, stuffing her pencil into the small back pocket. "Egg McMuffin, here I come."

Gary stood up and wiped his hands on his pants.

"Are you sure, Meg? We were just making some headway."

"That's okay," Megan said, rounding the couch to join Conner at the door. "Mac's a geometry god."

Gary locked eyes with Conner, and Conner couldn't help but smirk.

"C'mon! I'm salivating now," Megan said, pulling on Conner's wrist. "Thanks, Dad!"

"Have a good day!" Gary called as Conner and Megan headed through the foyer. As Conner opened the door for Megan and let her duck under his arm, he glanced over his shoulder and flashed a smile at Gary. The guy looked like a lost puppy.

So much for your headway, Conner thought.

Jessica Wakefield

<u>Reasons</u> <u>to</u> <u>Not</u> <u>Like</u> <u>Will</u>

1. He kissed me even though he already had a girlfriend — which is a jerk move. But it's also kind of romantic if he did it because he was so attracted to me that he couldn't stop himself.

2. He let me believe he really cared about me, and that makes him a total pig. Unless, of course, he really does.

3. He helped Melissa spread rumors about me and basically ruined the first part of my senior year. Although really he probably didn't help — he just didn't stop her right away. And he did clear everything up. Eventually.

4. Jeremy — he's the one I should really be with anyway. He's kind, sweet, funny, cute, smart, and totally perfect for me. And it shouldn't matter that my heart doesn't pound when I'm around him the way it does when I'm with Will. I still love being with him. But how can I count him as a reason when he doesn't even want to go out with me?

CHAPTER

What Was I Thinking?

7

Jessica plunked her cafeteria tray down on the industrial, rectangular table and took a seat directly across from her sister.

"What time is it?" she asked, her eyes drooping above a defeated frown.

"You've got five hours and fifty-eight minutes before the moment of truth," Elizabeth said, squinting at something just over Jessica's head. Jessica raised one eyebrow questioningly. "There's a clock behind you. How long have you been going to this school?" Elizabeth asked.

"Very funny," Jessica muttered.

"Thanks," Elizabeth said.

"How could you do this to me?" Jessica asked, dropping her head into her hands.

A loud cheer erupted from a table by the windows, and Jessica looked up to find the jock crowd giving itself an extremely self-satisfied standing ovation. Bruce Covington stood on a chair, throwing his beefy arms in the air in triumph. His face was covered with chocolate pudding, and Jessica could only imagine he had just broken some sugar-consuming record. Will stood up on the chair next to Bruce and grabbed his wrist, raising his arm even higher.

So mature. So attractive.

Jessica grimaced. "Maybe we'll have another earthquake or something," she said. "Or maybe I can turn his car lights on so his battery will die and he won't be able to get there. Ya think?"

Elizabeth exhaled sharply. "Oh, come on, Jessica. It's not that bad. So Will's coming over for dinner. What's the big deal?"

Jessica groaned and stared at the ceiling. "I don't know," she said helplessly. "I just can't believe you invited him. What were you thinking?"

"*You . . . like . . . him*," Elizabeth said, pronouncing each word slowly. She pushed aside her tray and leaned over the table. "Why don't you just admit it?"

"I do not," Jessica blurted out, sitting upright. She glanced at Will's killer smile again as he climbed down from his perch. "I just . . . Oh, I don't know," she moaned, closing her eyes tightly. When she opened them again, Elizabeth was gnawing at her apple distractedly and staring at the entrance to the cafeteria.

"I still don't see why everyone thinks I should just forgive him after all the things he said about me," Jessica said.

Elizabeth shrugged. "Probably because they realize that people make mistakes," she answered without taking her eyes off the door. "I mean, just because someone says something harsh, it doesn't necessarily mean that he all of a sudden doesn't care anymore."

Jessica felt like shaking her sister by the shoulders and screaming, *Not every conversation is about you and Conner!*

But part of what Elizabeth said was true. People did make mistakes. And it was Melissa and her friends who had done most of the public humiliating and rumor spreading.

"Besides," Elizabeth continued, glancing over Jessica's shoulder at the food line. "Andy thinks Will's okay."

Jessica turned around to see Andy approaching, his tray piled high with pizza. "Please," she begged in a low whisper, grabbing Elizabeth's wrist to get her sister's full attention. "Promise me you won't tell anyone that Will's coming over for dinner. I don't want it getting around to the whole school." *In other words, Melissa and her friends,* Jessica added silently.

"Um . . . oops?" Elizabeth said.

Feeling a heavy hand on her shoulder, Jessica sat upright to see Andy settling in next to her. "So," he said, unscrewing the top of his grape juice and looking at Jessica out of the corner of his eye. "Ready for your big date with Will?"

Someone was going to have to remind Jessica why she liked having a sister.

* * *

Conner searched the soccer field, concentrating on all the players in red and white, until he spotted Megan near the opposing team's goal. Good old number six. She'd chosen it because it was the number Conner had used when he played soccer back in middle school.

It had been a long time since Conner had attended one of Megan's games, but with everything going on lately, he figured the added support couldn't hurt.

"Let's go, Megan!" Conner yelled.

There was a skirmish, and for a moment he thought she might score, but then the goalie stepped in and sent the ball sailing through the air.

"Okay! It's okay! Keep on top of it!"

Conner turned toward the bleachers, checking to see if there was a big, open area where he could sit away from the other spectators. No such luck. He was about to turn away when he heard a familiar voice.

"Go, Megan!"

Oh, come on, Conner thought. *Not possible.* But sure enough, there was Gary, front and center, yelling through cupped hands. What was he doing here? But of course that seemed clear. He was busy pretending the last few years hadn't happened—that he wasn't the world's most accomplished absentee dad.

Conner turned back to the game, aware that if

Gary saw him, he'd have to go over and be civil so that Megan wouldn't be upset. Because of course if Conner saw Gary and didn't go over, Gary would make sure it was the main topic at dinner later.

Conner shoved his hands in his pockets and focused on the big digital clock across the field as it counted down the last five seconds of the first half. At the referee's whistle all the players slowed down and jogged over to their separate huddles.

"Hey! Conner!" Megan yelled, beaming as she approached the SVH bench. Conner nodded to her, feeling a sense of pride—and a small victory over Gary—that he had been addressed first. Megan said something to her coach and started to jog toward her brother. She was only fifteen feet away when she stopped in midstride.

"Dad!" Megan called, her face full of surprise as she switched directions and ran over to Gary instead. Conner swallowed hard, trying not to let his disappointment show. He watched as Megan threw her arms around Gary's shoulders and then turned proudly to a few of her teammates. "This is my father," he heard her say as Gary smiled and greeted them.

Conner felt an irritated flush rise to his face, but he tried to ignore it. He might as well let her enjoy it while it lasted. There was no way Conner was going to be the guy who rained on his sister's happy-family fantasy. Besides, he had a card up his sleeve. Conner took a deep breath and sauntered over to Megan and her father.

"Hey, Conner." Gary smiled, reaching over to clap Conner on the back as if he were greeting a long-lost friend. "Did you see your sister out there? Isn't she great?"

"Yeah," Conner said. "She always has been." He gave Gary a look that clearly said, "You'd know if you were ever around."

"Hey," Megan started, looking tentatively at her brother. "Dad's planning to take me and a few friends out for pizza after the game. Wanna come?"

Conner sucked in his breath, feeling like he had just been punched in the gut. So much for his hidden card. He had planned to take Megan and her two best friends out for ice cream after the game to make up for last night's argument with Gary at dinner.

He was about to tell her about his plan—leave it up to Megan to choose—but she looked so psyched, he didn't want to put her in an awkward position.

"Thanks, but I told Tia I'd hook up with her later," he lied. "She needed to talk." *At least that part's true,* he thought.

"Too bad," Gary said with a half smile. "I thought since pizza seems to be your preferred food group, you wouldn't be able to turn us down."

Conner wasn't about to dignify that one with anything more than a glare.

"Maybe next time?" Megan asked hopefully.

"Sure," Conner answered. He clenched his jaw, hating himself for lying to her and hating Gary even more for putting him in that position to begin with.

"Well, I've got to get back before Coach yells at me," Megan said, jogging away. "See you at home."

Conner watched her join the huddle, then glanced over at the stands. Even though Gary was looking the other way, Conner could swear he was gloating.

Next time, he thought bitterly, recalling what Megan had said. *Yeah, right. Mom will come home at the end of the month, and Gary will be out of here faster than she can say "Daddy."* Conner felt sick just thinking about it.

There wasn't going to be a next time.

The already familiar chimes of the new front doorbell sounded, sending Jessica's heart into hyperdrive.

Oh my God, oh my God, oh my God, she thought, taking one last look in the mirror.

"Jess-i-ca!" Mrs. Wakefield called from the kitchen. "Could you get that? It's probably your friend Will."

"My friend Will," Jessica muttered sarcastically. "And what are you looking at?" she asked her reflection. "This is not a date. You didn't even ask him."

"Jessica?" her mother prompted when the doorbell rang again.

"I got it!" Jessica shouted back, taking a deep breath and reminding herself to act cool. She stalked over to the front door and swung it open carelessly.

"Hi," Jessica said, trying hard to sound aloof as she focused on Will's brown loafers. *Loafers?* she wondered. Somehow she had expected to see the same battered boat shoes Will always wore at school. Her eyes lingered on his shoes, then drifted up his legs, along the creases of his neatly pressed, tan twill pants and crisp, white linen shirt. She allowed them to continue past the wide expanse of his shoulders and his clean-shaven jaw, finally resting on his bright blue-gray eyes.

"Hi." Will grinned. He'd just had mint gum.

Jessica swallowed hard, trying to control the muscles in the small of her back, which had begun twitching spasmodically.

"These are for you," Will said, drawing his left hand from behind his back to reveal a huge bouquet of deep blue irises.

"Wow," Jessica said with an involuntary gasp. She cleared her throat. "I mean, you shouldn't have. I'm not the one who invited you, remember?"

"Technically," Will said, silencing her with a smile. He brought his right arm forward and handed her a large box of chocolates wrapped in gold foil.

"Godiva," Jessica whispered, smiling in spite of herself. "I *love* these."

Will's grin broadened. "I know," he said.

"How?"

"You said so," Will explained with a shrug.

Jessica squinted. "I did? When?"

"Well, you didn't tell *me*," Will admitted, cocking his head. "It was in history, back on the first day of school. We all had to say our names and something about ourselves. . . ."

He can't possibly remember that, Jessica thought.

"You said you liked Ben & Jerry's ice cream and Godiva chocolates," Will finished.

"Oh," Jessica managed, blushing uncontrollably. She stood up on her toes and glanced over Will's shoulder. "You don't have ice cream out there too, do you?" she asked, half expecting him to produce a pint from his shirt pocket.

"No. Sorry." Will laughed, shaking his head. "I would have, but you never said what flavor." He might have been joking, but something told Jessica that if she mentioned chocolate chip cookie dough, a pint would show up in her freezer before the end of the night.

She opened the door wider and stepped aside. "So . . . come in," she said.

"Just a minute." Will bent down, reaching for something. Jessica's eyes widened when he stepped inside with a small potted plant he had stashed just outside the door. "This one's for your mom," Will said as Jessica ushered him into the family room. "Sort of a housewarming present and thanks-for-inviting-me-to-dinner gift."

"That's really nice . . . of you," Jessica said, feeling ridiculously formal. But she was so floored, she didn't know what else to say. She led him into the living room, where he sat down on the ecru love seat. Jessica hesitated for a split second and then perched on the edge of the sofa across from him.

Okay, so he's a polite dinner guest, she thought as he placed the plant on the coffee table. *But I hear Charles Manson is a real charmer too.*

"My mom will appreciate that," Jessica said, glancing at the plant as she put her gifts down next to her. "But you really didn't have to get me anything. I mean, it was my parents' idea to invite you over." It came out sounding a bit harsher than Jessica had intended, but she wanted to make it clear from the beginning that this wasn't a date.

Will didn't flinch. "I know," he said, tucking his chin and gazing up at her. "But I bet you're the one who'll decide whether or not I get invited back."

Jessica blinked, trying not to look away but feeling like she was going to say or do something stupid if she didn't.

"Um, I'm going to let everyone know you're here," she said, standing abruptly and practically running to the kitchen. *I am* not *attracted to him,* she repeated to herself with each step, eyeing the goose bumps on her upper arms. *I'm just cold.* Jessica rubbed at her skin with a sweaty palm. *Or something.*

"Where's Will?" Mrs. Wakefield asked the second Jessica had both feet through the doorway. "Wasn't that him at the door?"

"Yeah. He's in the living room," Jessica answered, pointing her thumb over her shoulder. She headed straight for the refrigerator, ignoring her mother's watchful eye. Filling a glass with ice water from the freezer door, she downed it in one gulp.

"Are you okay?" Mrs. Wakefield asked, her forehead creased with concern.

"Yeah," Jessica said. She turned to refill her glass. "It's just hot in here."

Mrs. Wakefield finished stirring the vegetables on the stove and turned off the burner. "No hotter than usual," she said over her shoulder. "Do you feel sick?"

Yes, but it's not a fever, Jessica thought as she leaned back against the refrigerator. "No, I'm fine."

Mrs. Wakefield closed the oven door. "Jessica?" she said, lifting her eyebrows. "Don't you think you should see if *Will* wants something to drink?"

Jessica jostled her glass, spilling a drop of water down the front of her pink halter dress. "Damn," she muttered under her breath, snatching a dishcloth from above the sink and dabbing at her clothes. Great. Now she was incoherent *and* sloppy. "I mean, yeah. I guess I should," she said.

"And why don't you ask him to come in here and sit down so we can all talk?" Mrs. Wakefield added as she began sweeping crumbs from the counter with one hand.

Jessica threw the cloth in the sink and looked at her mother, smiling weakly. "Okay," she said, knowing that if she avoided going back into the living room for too long, her mother was going to start with the probing questions. At least she wouldn't have to be alone with him anymore.

But before Jessica left the room, Elizabeth came in with Will at her side.

"Jeez, Jess," Elizabeth said, frowning at her sister. "Will's been sitting in there alone for ten minutes. No wonder your friends don't visit more often."

Jessica glared as Elizabeth walked over to the stove and picked a pea pod out of the frying pan. Elizabeth was the one who should be playing hostess, considering she was brilliant enough to invite the guy over.

"Elizabeth," Mrs. Wakefield whispered harshly. "Why don't you get the cheese plate from the refrigerator and set it out with some crackers?" Elizabeth rolled her eyes and grudgingly obeyed while Mrs. Wakefield looked back at Will and smiled.

"Hi, Will," she said warmly. "It's nice to see you again."

"You too, Mrs. Wakefield. Thanks for inviting me." Will held the plant out to her. "This is for you."

Jessica's mother smiled broadly. "Oh, thank you. How thoughtful," she said, sneaking a look at Jessica.

It was the "hold-on-to-this-one" look. Just perfect.

"Thanks again for all your help on Sunday," Mrs. Wakefield continued, placing the gift on the counter. "We were lucky you came along. I wish Jessica and her sister had more friends like you."

Unbelievable. Was she going to save any enthusiasm for the wedding day? Jessica crossed her arms over her chest and scowled at Will.

"Actually, Mrs. Wakefield—"

"Call me Alice," Jessica's mother said, eliciting an eye roll from Jessica.

Will chuckled. "Okay. *Alice*," he started. Jessica smirked, secretly pleased that using her mother's first name seemed to make Will uncomfortable. It was about time something made him sweat a little. Will cleared his throat. "I was just going to say that *I* wouldn't mind having more friends like Jessica."

A slight smile played at the corner of her mother's mouth. "Oh?" she asked.

Jessica's shoulders tensed. She sensed that another onslaught of Will charm was about to begin.

"Yeah." Will nodded, his incredibly gorgeous Matt Damon–esque grin lighting up his entire face. "But I get the feeling she's one of a kind."

Jessica was sure she was going to vomit on the newly tiled kitchen floor. She looked at her mother, waiting for her to drop to her knees and kiss Will's feet for being such a gentleman.

But instead Mrs. Wakefield smirked. "Pouring it

125

on a little thick, aren't we?" she said dryly. Jessica's heart dropped, but she couldn't have wiped the grin off her face if she tried. It was all she could do to keep from hugging her mother in pride.

Of course, Will just laughed it off. "Well, you gotta try," he said, shrugging. Did nothing affect this guy?

"I understand," Mrs. Wakefield said with a laugh, patting him on the back. "Why don't we go join Liz in the living room?"

Jessica followed Will and her mom through the kitchen door. She wasn't surprised when her mother turned around and mouthed the words "I *like* him," followed by a big grin. Of course she did. She'd called him on his butt kissing, and he'd readily admitted it. Jessica's mom loved nothing more than honesty.

Apparently Will was made out of Teflon. Nothing he did wrong stuck to him. It just slid away, and he kept coming out looking fresh and new and incredibly gorgeous.

Her mother was completely taken in.

Unfortunately, Jessica thought as Will reclaimed his place on the love seat and gazed up at her, *Mom's not the only one.*

TIA RAMIREZ

<u>REASONS</u> <u>TO</u> <u>DO</u> <u>IT</u>

I LOVE HIM.

HE LOVES ME.

IT WOULD BE AMAZING.

I WANT HIM TO BE MY FIRST.

I WANT TO BE HIS FIRST.

HE'LL REMEMBER ME WHEN HE LEAVES.

(EVERYONE SAYS YOU NEVER FORGET

YOUR FIRST TIME.)

<u>REASONS</u> <u>NOT</u> <u>TO</u> <u>DO</u> <u>IT</u>

I'M NOT SURE I'M READY.

I'M NOT SURE HE'S READY.

I'M KIND OF SCARED.

WHAT IF I'M NOT GOOD AT IT?

WHAT IF HE'S NOT GOOD AT IT?

WE HAVEN'T TALKED ABOUT BIRTH CONTROL.

MY DAD WOULD KILL ME.

MY MOM WOULD KILL ME—TWICE.

READY WHEN YOU ARE

Conner sat down on his bed and was just about to put on his headphones when Megan burst into his room and did a belly flop onto his mattress.

"Hey, Conner," she said, beaming as he bounced from the force of her dive. "You really should have come with us tonight. It was so fun."

That's Gary, the king of fun, Conner thought. "Good," he said, nodding as he strummed a chord.

Megan either didn't notice his lack of enthusiasm or chose to ignore it. "We went to Pete's Pizza Palace over in Ridgewood and then out for ice cream after. It was great. All my friends were *so* jealous. Erin Martin even told me she wished her father were as cool as mine." She giggled and rolled over on her back while Conner studied her face. *She hasn't looked this happy since . . . since the day Liz moved in,* he thought, refusing to dwell on the idea. He was too alarmed by Megan's sudden attachment to her father to think about Elizabeth.

"That's great, Sandy," he said, wondering if it was safe to say anything else.

She pulled a lock of her hair in front of her face and started to braid it, practically going cross-eyed from concentrating. "I bet Dad'll come to a lot of my basketball games too. I think I have a chance at varsity."

Conner's stomach was turning again. Gary hadn't come to a single game last year. What made Megan think this season would be different? "It'd probably be tough for him to come down from Seattle for weekday games," Conner said, trying not to sound *too* negative.

"Not if he moves back to California," Megan said.

Conner sucked in a breath, and Megan dropped her hair to look up at him.

"What?" she prompted.

Trying with all his strength to keep from shaking, Conner placed his guitar down on the floor in front of him and stared at the strings. "What makes you think Gary's moving back to California?"

"He said he might," Megan said, sitting up so that her legs swung right next to Conner's. "He said he missed the sun and the weather and everything."

Conner's mind was a blur of random thoughts. *He said he might.* Was Gary really thinking about coming back? Not likely. He had a practice up in Seattle, and if there was one thing Gary was always up front about, it was that his career came first. The jerk was just leading Megan on. It was bad enough watching her get close to Gary, but if he got her hopes up—

"Really I think he just misses me," Megan said with a smile that made Conner's heart shatter.

He was going to kill Gary.

"Megan, it's not that simple for people to just drop their lives and move around," Conner said slowly.

"I know," Megan said. She stood up and crossed over to Conner's desk, where she started fiddling with a tape dispenser he'd never touched in his life. "I'm just telling you what he told me."

"He said he was moving back?" Conner asked, leaning back on his elbows.

Megan sighed in exasperation. "He said he was *thinking* about it." She dropped the tape dispenser and moved on to a book of Bob Dylan songs, flipping through the pages without seeing a thing. "But I think he will. We've been having a lot of fun together." She looked up at him as if she was gauging his reaction. Conner kept his face as expressionless as possible, but inside he was fuming.

We've been having a lot of fun together. So Megan thought Gary's decision to move hinged on whether or not he enjoyed Megan's company. And when Gary decided to keep the responsibility-free life in Seattle, Megan would think it was because she had somehow failed.

"Plus I think he might still care about Mom," Megan said. "He said he missed her."

"What!" Conner shouted, standing up. His face

was so hot, he was sure there was fire spilling out of his pores. "Did he *tell* you that too?"

Megan's eyes were wide. "Conner—"

"So. What? Now you think we're all going to be one big, happy family?"

"Conner, calm down."

The word *calm* was no longer in Conner's vocabulary. "Where is he?" Conner asked through clenched teeth.

"What're you going to do?" Megan asked, clutching the songbook as if it were a long-lost teddy bear.

"Just tell me where he is," Conner demanded.

"He's out back," Megan said. "I think he's reading on the lawn. . . ."

Conner was out the door and down the stairs before she even finished her sentence. He'd kept quiet long enough.

Tia sat on the front steps at Angel's house, wondering if the pattern of the grainy concrete she was sitting on was going to be permanently imprinted in her thighs. Angel's parents were out, and it was already dark. Angel was supposed to get out of work an hour ago, and in the past sixty minutes of waiting, Tia had gone from queasy to nervous to tense to bored.

Suddenly she heard the familiar sound of his car's gasping engine and was on her feet in a flash, her heart slamming against her rib cage. This was it. The moment of truth.

"Hey, baby!" Angel called as he climbed out of his car. "What are you—"

But Tia didn't let him finish his sentence. She jogged over to him, threw her arms around his neck, and planted a big kiss on his surprised lips.

"I was beginning to wonder if you were coming back," she said in a low, husky voice, pulling back ever so slightly.

"Well, if I had known about this, I would've been here hours ago," Angel said in a seductive tone. He kissed her again, deeply, sending shivers down Tia's back. When she peeked at Angel, a lazy smile had spread across his lips.

"Whatever I did to deserve this, I'm going to have to start doing a lot more of it," he said. He squeezed her tightly before letting her go. "Let's go inside," he said, suddenly sounding excited. "I want to talk to you where I can see your beautiful face."

"How could I possibly say no to that?" Tia smiled, grasping his hand and following him into the house. Angel took off his coat and hung it on the wooden hooks next to the door, then led her into the living room.

"So . . . we're all alone," Tia said suggestively, glancing around as Angel turned on the lights.

"And that means I can tell you the good news first," he said, grinning.

Tia's heart skipped a beat and landed with a thud. All thoughts of seduction flew out the window with her composure. "You got the job?" she asked, somewhere between panicked and pleased.

"Well, not exactly," Angel answered, plopping onto the sofa.

Tia walked over and sat next to him, tucking one leg beneath her. She turned so she could face him. "What do you mean?"

"When I first got there, they almost sent me home," he started, picking up her hand and entwining his fingers with hers. "They said they'd reviewed my application and realized I was only going to be a freshman, and they don't let new students become RAs until at least their second semester."

"That's annoying," Tia said. "I don't even remember seeing that on the application."

"I know," Angel said, his brown eyes wide. "But it kind of makes sense when you think about it. Anyway, it doesn't matter."

"It doesn't?" Tia asked as she watched his face light up all over again.

"Well, it turns out they have this peer-adviser position that has all the same perks but not as much actual responsibility. It's almost like training to be an RA," Angel explained. "So I interviewed for that one instead, and I think I really nailed it. It was awesome."

"Angel, that's great!" Tia said, leaning forward to hug him. "You must have been freaking when they said you were too young."

"Definitely," Angel said, hugging her back. "But it looks like I'll be able to go to college after all."

Tia grinned, pushing aside the sick feeling she got every time he talked about leaving. She pulled back and looked him in the eye. "Have I told you recently that I love you?" she asked.

"Not in the past few minutes," Angel said with a heart-stopping smile. He leaned back against the soft couch cushions and pulled Tia to him so that she was leaning against his chest. Her heart was pounding crazily as she pressed her lips to his, then cuddled into him. He held her tightly in his arms, his kisses intense.

He feels the same way I do, Tia thought. *He wants me too.*

Angel broke away and started to trail tiny kisses down her neck, running his fingers through her hair. Tia kept her eyes closed and felt nothing but the sensation of his lips against her skin. It felt so perfect. He felt so perfect.

"I love you," she said again.

"You said that already," he said huskily before pressing his lips to hers again. She kissed him gently at first, then pressing harder, trying to communicate her feelings—show him what she wanted.

Maybe I should whisper it in his ear, she thought, her heart practically stopping at the thought. But what would she say? How would she say it?

She was beginning to wish that she'd paid more

attention to the love scenes in all the movies she'd seen recently. Slowly Tia kissed her way across Angel's cheek and over to his ear, but when she got there, she lost her nerve and started to nibble lightly on his earlobe.

"Hey!" Angel said, laughing as he pulled away. "What are you doing?"

Obviously not the right thing, Tia thought, feeling like a total idiot. "Nothing," she answered defensively, her stomach turning. "Did I hurt you?"

Angel chuckled and casually ran his hands down her back. "No, actually it kind of tickled."

It tickled. Great. Somehow that didn't sound very sexy.

"Oh," Tia said, looking down at his chest. "Well, did it feel . . . you know . . . good?"

Angel put his finger under her chin and tilted up her face, forcing her to look him in the eye. "Yeah. Of course it did." He planted a kiss on the tip of her nose. "Tia, are you okay?"

Apparently not when it comes to sex, she thought. Tia glanced up at him, too embarrassed to explain what she was really thinking. "Yeah. Why?"

Angel shook his head and shrugged. "No reason," he said, sounding only half convincing.

This is just lovely, Tia thought sarcastically. *I try to turn my boyfriend on, and he assumes I'm not feeling well.*

"Oh, hey," Angel said, putting an end to the

awkward silence. "Did I mention that I should know by tomorrow whether or not I got the job?" he asked.

Interesting segue. Straight from kissing to college. It didn't say much for her smooching ability. A sickening thought occurred to her, and she tried not to squirm. Maybe she and Angel had been together for so long that she just wasn't exciting to him anymore.

"No, you didn't," she said, her tone flat. "That's pretty quick."

Angel scrutinized her face again, and she knew her lack of enthusiasm was obvious.

"Are you sure you're okay?" he asked. "You seem . . . preoccupied or something."

That was the understatement of the century. Tia bit her lip. "Well . . . I guess there is something that's kind of been on my mind lately," she started.

Angel shifted slightly, sitting up straighter so that Tia was nestled in the crook of his arm.

"What's up?" he asked, running his finger down her cheekbone.

"I was just wondering . . . Well, don't you ever think about . . . ?" She raised her eyebrows, hoping he would just get it so she wouldn't have to say it.

Angel chuckled. "Tia? What's going on with you?"

"I'm just asking," Tia said, staring up at the ceiling. "It doesn't help that you keep laughing at me, you know," she told him.

"I'm sorry," Angel apologized quickly. "It's just that . . . Where is this coming from? I thought we decided a long time ago that we'd wait and talk about it more when we were both ready."

"Well," Tia said, trying to sound casual. "I'm ready."

Angel just looked at her. She watched his eyes go from shocked to psyched to something she couldn't read at all. Her heart squeezed. This was not a good sign.

"Since when?" he said finally.

"I don't know," Tia mumbled, lifting one shoulder. "Since . . . What does it matter?" she asked defensively. "I just feel like I'm ready."

"Well, don't you think maybe we should talk about it some more before you start devouring my ear?" he said in a lame attempt at levity.

Tia exhaled sharply. "Come on, it's not funny. I was just trying to . . ." Tia scowled at him and started fidgeting with the couch cushion. "Besides—it's not like we have a whole lot of time to talk about it. You're leaving on—"

Suddenly Angel's entire body stiffened. He pulled his arm from behind her head and slid a few inches away.

"Is that what this is about?" Angel asked.

No, Tia thought. *The correct answer here would be no.* She opened her mouth to explain herself, but she was too confused to form a coherent response.

Angel reached over and took both of her hands in his, looking at her tenderly. "Tia, you have to know by now that you've got nothing to worry about. A few extra miles between us isn't going to change anything." Tia tried to listen, but tears were already forming in the corners of her eyes. "And when we do make love, I want it to be because you want me—not because you're afraid of losing me."

His voice was tender and soothing, and his eyes were full of concern, but there was still a feeling that Tia couldn't shake. A feeling that she was already losing him.

"I *do* want you," she said. "I *love* you." She spoke the words slowly—urgently—while she examined Angel's face for the one emotion that seemed to be missing.

"I love you too, Tia. But I think we should wait," Angel said.

He looked into her eyes, but it wasn't there. He didn't want her.

Oh my God, Tia thought, blinking. *I might as well be his sister. He doesn't want me—he feels sorry for me.*

She stood up and headed for the door, pulling her hands away from Angel even as he tried to hold on to her.

"That was a great dinner, Mrs. Wakefield—I mean, *Alice,*" Will said, standing to help clear the dishes from the table.

Jessica could tell he was still a little uncomfortable with the whole first-name thing, and she couldn't help but smile. The way he stumbled on it each time was actually kind of cute.

"Thank you, Will," Mrs. Wakefield answered, clearly amused.

Jessica started to get up, but Will took her plate and stacked it on top of his, gesturing for her to sit down. Before Jessica could speak, Will had grabbed Elizabeth's as well, along with a few napkins.

"Please, Will, just sit and relax," Mr. Wakefield said as he started toward the kitchen. "We can clear."

"That's okay, uh—*Ned*," Will said, causing Jessica to smirk. "I don't mind. My mom always makes me do it at home, so I'm pretty used to it." He glanced at Jessica on his way out, raising his eyebrows and smiling.

"You've gotta like that," Jessica whispered to Elizabeth. "Most guys just sit there, you know? Like at Thanksgiving, how Uncle Lou and Grandpa always just wait for the women to clear. I *hate* that."

"I guess," Elizabeth said, shrugging disinterestedly as she stood up and pushed in her chair.

Jessica bit her tongue. You'd think that since Elizabeth was the one who had invited Will in the first place, she'd have *some* interest in what was going on around her. But it seemed Elizabeth was back in the Conner-centered universe. If the conversation didn't include the words *McDermott,*

Sandborn, or *forgiveness,* it didn't matter.

Jessica stood up and followed her sister's lead, taking the remaining dishes into the kitchen. But as soon as she entered the room, her mother grabbed her by the elbow and pulled her toward the pantry.

"Will's great, Jessica," she said, her blue eyes shining. "Your father and I really like him."

Jessica smiled, feeling strangely proud, as if she had just won some kind of parental-approval award. *Wait a second,* she thought. *Why do I want their approval? Approval of what?*

"I thought he was nice when I met him on Sunday," Mrs. Wakefield continued, "but I can't remember when either of you brought home a guy who was this polite and mature."

Jessica laughed. "Thanks, Mom," she said, glancing over at Will as he scraped each dish and passed it to her father. "Yeah. I guess he scored a few points tonight."

"More. like a few hundred," Mrs. Wakefield said with a knowing smile. "All right, Will," she called out. "You've done enough. Why don't you and Jessica go hang out in the living room?"

"I don't mind helping," Will said, glancing at Jessica. She just smiled and looked away.

"We know. It's okay," Mrs. Wakefield said, patting his shoulder. "You're the guest."

"Does this mean I get out of dish duty too?" Jessica asked, raising her eyebrows.

"Only if you get out of here in the next five seconds," her mother answered. Jessica immediately grabbed Will by the arm and ushered him through the door.

When they reached the living room, Jessica took a seat on the sofa and Will returned to the love seat. Jessica couldn't help noticing that they were in the exact positions they had been in at the beginning of the night, but now things felt entirely different.

"I should have people over for dinner more often," Jessica joked.

Will laughed. "So that's why you invited me. To get out of doing the dishes."

Jessica shrugged. "It's definitely a perk," she said, not bothering to remind him once again that she had nothing to do with his being here. She held Will's eyes for a moment but couldn't keep herself from blushing under his cool, confident gaze.

It wasn't fair. He seemed to get more confident every time Jessica got more neurotic. She looked at the end table, feigning interest in a couple of framed photographs her mother had managed to unpack in honor of Will's visit.

"Isn't this kind of weird?" she said, picking up one of the picture frames and turning it toward Will. It contained two pictures side by side—one of her at age three, holding a big blue ball, and one of Elizabeth at the same age, doing the same thing. "I mean, if you didn't know I had a twin sister, you'd just think there were two pictures of me doing everything all over the house." She laughed nervously and tried to set the frame back down but misjudged the distance to the table and ended up scratching it loudly across the wood. "Oops," she said, trying not to let on just how mortified she felt. There was no way she could possibly be more lame.

"Jessica," Will said, leaning forward with his elbows resting on his knees and his hands clasped.

"Yeah?" Jessica squeaked. Just hearing him pronounce her name in his husky voice made her tingle all over.

"I was just wondering . . ." Will took a deep breath and narrowed his eyes as he watched her. Jessica looked back at him, her nerves jittery as she wondered what he was about to say. "What do you think it is that makes you so nervous around me?"

Jessica swallowed hard. "Nervous?" she asked, smiling weakly. "What makes you think I'm nervous?" *The way my voice is shaking?*

Will smiled, a playful look dancing through his eyes. "I don't know," he said, standing and walking toward her. "The way you keep avoiding looking at me, or maybe just the fact that you keep sitting so far away." He edged his way around the coffee table and sat down beside her.

"I can look at you," Jessica said, forcing herself to hold his gaze, but as Will continued to move closer, she couldn't help blinking rapidly and darting her eyes over his shoulder. "Did you hear that?" she said, hoping he'd turn around to look.

But Will didn't move. "No," he said, shaking his head slowly.

"Oh. Well, I th-thought I heard something," Jessica stammered. "Maybe I should go check. It could be the . . . neighbors' dog. Sometimes he gets . . . out."

What the hell am I talking about? she thought, getting ready to stand up.

"Don't," Will said, placing one hand on her thigh.

Jessica's breath caught in her throat. She was surprised to find herself both scared and excited by the throbbing of her leg underneath Will's palm. "Will . . . my parents."

"I think they went upstairs," he said, looking over her shoulder toward the kitchen.

Jessica listened and realized the clatters and running water and murmured voices had ceased. Were her parents insane? Did they think that just because Will had cleared a few plates, it was okay to leave their daughter alone with him? What kind of parents were they?

You're panicking, Jessica told herself. *Stop.*

"Still—"

"Okay." Will slowly pulled his hand away, never breaking eye contact. He rested his arm on the back of the couch and leaned a little bit closer.

"There's something I've been wanting to tell you for a long time," he said, looking deep into her eyes.

Jessica tried to swallow, but her throat was dry. Her heart pounded in anticipation.

"I didn't want to say anything until things were settled with Melissa, but I wanted to break up with her at the beginning of the year—the minute I met you. It was just . . . I knew what would happen if I did." He sighed and gently tucked a strand of hair behind her ear. Jessica could feel the warmth of his breath as he spoke. "So I just stayed—way too long."

His hand grazed her bare shoulder until he rested his thumb there, making slow circles that seemed to pulse throughout her body. This time she didn't tell him to stop.

"But now," he said quietly, "Melissa's out of the picture."

"Um," Jessica said, lowering her eyelids. Somehow she wanted to press herself into him and run away all at once.

Will moved closer still, his face only inches away now. "I want you to go out with me," he whispered, lowering his head to catch her eyes. "On a date."

Jessica looked up at him, her mind swimming and dizzy. "I don't know," she started. "I just . . ."

Will smiled, a mischievous twinkle in his eye. "I know why you get so nervous around me," he said, his voice barely audible.

"You do?" Jessica whispered. She was on the verge of hyperventilating.

A wicked grin played across Will's face as he moved close enough for Jessica to feel his lips graze hers when he spoke. "Yeah," he said. "You remember that first kiss."

"Mm-hmm," Jessica whimpered. She closed her eyes, unable to hold back any longer. She leaned into him, pressing her lips against his and feeling all of her original desire for him burst through her veins. Will deepened the kiss, then pushed her back gently, resting his forehead against hers. His breathing was slightly off.

"So will you go out with me?" he asked, his voice low and gravelly.

"Uh-huh," Jessica said, letting out her breath with the words.

And she'd never been more sure of anything.

Angel Desmond

I don't get it. Usually I know what Tia's thinking before she does, but this time she's got me totally confused. I mean, you'd think she'd be glad that I want to wait until we're both ready—really ready—to have sex. A lot of guys would have taken advantage of the situation, but not me, and not because I'm some kind of saint or anything 'cause I'm not.

It's because I love her.

And she knows that.

So what's going on?

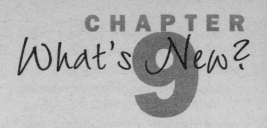
Conner burst through the back door of the house, flinging the glass door so that it slammed into the outside wall. He was surprised and not a little bit disappointed when the glass didn't shatter. He felt like breaking things.

Gary was lying on a chaise lounge, reading a newspaper. He sat up straight when he saw Conner coming across the patio toward him. For a gratifying moment Conner thought he saw fear behind Gary's eyes. No wonder, considering Conner probably looked like a crazed lunatic. But in a flash the fear was gone and that infuriating detached calmness had returned to Gary's face.

"Conner," he said.

"What the *hell* do you think you're doing?" Conner shouted, hovering right above Gary.

Megan stepped out onto the patio, and Conner saw her open her mouth to speak.

"Sandy, get back inside," Conner said. He looked her directly in the eye, trying to ignore the slack paleness of her skin. "Now."

Megan turned on her heel and disappeared into the house. She was a stubborn girl, but she knew when it was safer to stay away from Conner. Now was definitely one of those moments.

"What seems to be the problem, Conner?" Gary asked, rising to his feet and crossing his pudgy arms across his chest. Even at full height Gary was a few inches shorter than Conner—a basic advantage that didn't escape Conner's attention.

"You told Megan you were moving back to California," Conner said, his fists clenched at his sides, his elbows slightly bent as if he were ready to let fly at any provocation. "You told her you *missed* my mother."

"Now, I—"

"What's the matter, Gary? Didn't get enough money in the first divorce?" Conner spat. Gary's usually ruddy face drained of color, and the uncertainty was back in his eyes. Score one for Conner. "I'm not going to let you use my sister to get more of my mom's cash."

Gary's beady eyes squinted up even smaller. "Is that what you think the divorce was all about?"

Conner was surprised to hear himself laugh. He didn't think it was possible at that moment. "Everyone knows you only married my mother for her family's money. I don't know why you thought you had to have a kid, but I'm not going to let you hurt her any more, and I—"

"That's enough!" Gary exploded. Conner's mouth snapped shut, and he narrowed his eyes.

Gary turned around, bringing a hand to his forehead, then quickly turned on Conner again. "I am not going to let you stand here and tell me I don't love my daughter," he said, his face flushing again.

"You left her, and you hardly ever call," Conner said flatly. "Funny definition of love."

"I'm not saying I'm the father of the year," Gary said. He slowly lowered himself onto the long, flat part of the chaise, and Conner noticed he was shaking. He took a step back, irritated by Gary's display of weakness. Conner much preferred yelling to quiet discussion. "But there were complications when your mother and I divorced."

Gary looked up at Conner, searching his face as if he were wondering what to spill and what not to spill. "Your mother was already drinking," he said. "She made threats."

Conner felt his face grow red, and he fought for control, breathing slowly and concentrating on the swaying palm at the edge of the yard. "You're going to blame this on my mother?"

"I'm not blaming this on anyone," Gary said with a sigh. "But I didn't lie when I told Megan I was thinking of moving back. And I didn't lie when I said I missed your mother. In hindsight, yes, maybe I shouldn't have said it, but it wasn't a lie."

This was vomit inducing. The guy still cared

about Conner's mother? Did he actually want to get back together with her? Conner had to push that thought aside before he threw up all over Gary's shoes. Talk about a sign of weakness. That would definitely kill his credibility.

Glaring down at Gary, Conner asked the one question he knew he didn't want the answer to. "What kind of threats?"

"She was sick, Conner," Gary said. "I don't blame her, and you shouldn't either."

"What . . . kind . . . of threats?" Conner repeated.

"I don't think we should talk about this anymore," Gary said, rubbing his hands over his temples. "This is for you and your mother to discuss."

"You brought it up," Conner spat. "Just tell me."

"No, Conner," Gary said. "I've already said more than I should."

Conner rolled back his shoulders, pulling himself up to his full height. "Fine. I'll just find out for myself," he said, turning and starting back toward the house.

"Don't go calling your mother!" Gary called after him. "She shouldn't be upset!"

As he closed the door against Gary's shouts, Conner took a long, deep breath. He had no intention of talking to his mother. There was no way he could ever trust that he'd get a straight answer out of her.

There were other, more reliable ways of finding out the truth.

*   *   *

"Three lattes, two chocolate-chip cookies, and a chocolate-almond biscotti," Jessica said, passing everything over the counter.

The customer thanked her and joined her friends at a table near the door. Jessica looked around House of Java nervously. It was the moment she'd been dreading. The evening rush was over, but there was still an hour to closing, and she was stuck behind the counter with Jeremy.

A week or two ago it would have been her dream shift, but now that she and Jeremy were history, she felt desperate for customers to fill the awkward silence. Jeremy finished replacing the sugar at the tables and came over to start cleaning off the espresso machine. Jessica moved to the other end of the counter and began cramming napkins into the already full holders, trying to look busy. It didn't work.

"So," Jeremy said, throwing his cloth over his shoulder and leaning back against the green countertop. "How have you been?"

"Fine," Jessica answered, her voice fluttering nervously. She looked into Jeremy's brown eyes, unable to shake the feeling that she had betrayed him somehow—even though he was the one who insisted they spend some time apart.

"Uh, this might sound strange . . . you know . . . considering," Jeremy said, "but my dad gave me two tickets to some play for Saturday night, and I was wondering . . . if you want them."

Jessica lost all powers of speech.

"I don't mean that you have to go with *me* or anything," Jeremy said quickly. "It's just that I don't think I can use them, and I thought maybe you and Liz would want to go or something. . . ."

He looked like he was about to be ill.

"Thanks," Jessica said, her voice dry and raspy. "But I, um . . . already have plans." *Please don't ask me what I'm doing,* she thought, turning back to the napkin holder as if it were an urgent chore.

"Oh." Jeremy cleared his throat, and she could tell he wanted to know. His entire body was tense. He opened his mouth to speak, and Jessica held her breath.

"How is Liz anyway?" Jeremy said. "I haven't seen her in a while."

Jessica sighed slowly.

"She's fine," she said, staring down at her fingers.

"Well . . . anyway, tell her I said hi," Jeremy said, taking the cloth from his shoulder. He turned and began wiping down the already gleaming countertop, and Jessica felt a guilty ache in the pit of her stomach.

Why do I feel like I'm cheating on him? she thought, hanging her head and sighing. *It's not like he's my boyfriend anymore. I don't have to explain myself to him.* But as she watched him rub feverishly at a spot that wasn't there, she couldn't help feeling that *not* telling him about Will was a kind of deception too.

What if he found out about it some other way? Like through Melissa. When Jessica and Will had met to plan the kidnap breakfast, Melissa had told Jeremy they were on a date, and that was what had caused all their problems in the first place. Jessica had to tell him the truth now. There was no way she wanted to go through all that confusion again.

Jessica walked slowly over to Jeremy, her heart cold and heavy, but determined. He was occupying himself by straightening the towers of large white mugs and dessert plates.

"Listen," she said, hoping that maybe lightning would strike her and render her mute, just for a little while. "There's something I need to . . . tell you."

Jeremy looked over his shoulder, and Jessica could tell he wanted to flee. He wasn't stupid. He could tell from her tone that she wasn't about to make a happy announcement. Best to get it over with.

"It's about my plans for Saturday night," she said, looking past him at a crack in the brick wall. Now he was holding his breath. "I have a date," she finally managed, forcing herself to look at him. "With Will."

Jeremy's face went blank. "Oh," he said. He held her gaze for about two seconds, then looked down at his feet. "You know . . . I . . . uh . . . I think I left the phone off the hook in the back," he said, smiling weakly. "I better go check." He turned quickly and pushed the swinging door that led to the back room so hard, it slammed into the wall behind it.

"That went well," Jessica muttered as she leaned forward on the counter. She glanced back at the door, which was still swinging. "Compared to the last scene of *Titanic*."

She cradled her chin in her hands and closed her eyes, sighing heavily. *I hope I know what I'm doing.*

Conner clutched a piece of expensive law-office stationery in his hand and read the same line for the fiftieth time.

> *Pursuant to your conversation with Mr. Gary T. Sandborn of October the ninth, we have decided to discontinue our suit for custody of minor Megan Eleanore Sandborn.*

This was unbelievable. It was not possible. But there it was, in black and white, backed up by pages and pages of official documents.

Gary had fought for custody of Megan for months. He'd actually wanted her to live with him. Somehow that part of the story had never entered into his mother's version of the divorce. Conner and Megan had been kept out of the proceedings. While papers were being filed and lawyers were calling at all hours of the night, his mother had refused to answer any of her children's questions.

But when it was over . . . Well, then they'd gotten

an earful. All Gary cared about was the money. All he wanted was cash to start up a new practice in Seattle. He never cared about Conner's mother. He never cared about any of them.

Conner leaned back against the flower-papered wall in his mother's room. There were documents of all thicknesses and lengths strewn all around him and an open file box at his side. It had taken him about five seconds to find the "hidden" files. About five more seconds to bust open the lock.

About five more seconds to realize he knew nothing about his family.

Conner leaned forward and started stuffing papers back into the file box, his actions becoming more and more violent as he worked. He slammed the box shut and practically threw it into his mother's closet, where it landed with an unsatisfying thud.

Pushing his hands through his hair, Conner sat down on the bed and tried to clear his mind long enough to think. Gary did love Megan. Or at least wanted her. That much was obvious, but it wasn't easy for Conner to swallow. If there was one thing Conner had been certain about all this time, it was that Gary couldn't care less about his daughter. The new info was going to take a while to process.

And it seemed as if his mother *had* threatened Gary. But threatened him with what?

Conner stared at the closed bedroom door as if

his mother were going to walk in and explain every-thing. But that was never going to happen. He wasn't even sure he wanted it to.

Lying back on the bed, Conner closed his eyes and took a deep breath. So Gary was two for two. He'd said he cared about Megan and that there were threats. Conner had documented proof of both. She'd obviously said something to Gary during the "conversation" the letter alluded to. Something that had made him drop the custody battle.

So Gary was telling the truth. But he'd also said he'd cared about Conner's mother. That he missed her. Was that true too? If his mother got sober, would Gary . . . want her back?

Conner pressed his eyes together even tighter, pressing the heel of his hand against his forehead. The thought of his mother and Gary reconciling practically gave him vertigo. But he couldn't think about that now. There were more immediate stomach-shifting thoughts to consider.

Like the fact that he was wrong. And the fact that he was going to have to call a truce with Gary. It was time for peace among the McDermott/Sandborns.

Megan's life had been messed with enough al-ready.

Jeremy Aames

Jeremy—
I'm working on the order for the supply company. Can you make a note of anything you notice we're running low on?
                    Thanks,
                    Ally

Let's see . . .
money
pride
dignity
self-worth
a love life . . .

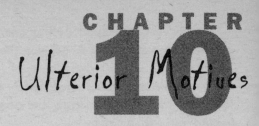
Tia was just about to slip out of her robe and into the soothing warm bath she'd been looking forward to all day when the doorbell rang.

"Great," Tia muttered. "The one time the million people who live here are all out." So much for leaning back and meditating on what to do about Angel. Tia had even been prepared for a long, heart-wrenching cry if that was what her body decided it needed.

She retied her robe and glanced forlornly at the bubbles in the tub. She should have known it was too good to be true.

Trudging down the stairs, Tia quickly rehearsed what she would say to whoever was at the door. "Sorry, we don't want any. . . . No, I don't want to join your new revisionist cult, thank you. . . . Go away, Conner, I no longer feel like talking."

Suddenly Tia caught a glimpse of black hair through the window. Her heart responded before she even registered who it was.

"Angel?" she said aloud, pulling open the wooden door at the same time Angel got the screen one. "What are—"

"Why haven't you called me?" Angel asked, squeezing past her and letting the door swing shut behind him with a bang.

"I—I've been busy," Tia stammered, following him into the living room.

Angel stopped in the middle of the toy-strewn floor and turned to face her, his arms crossed over his chest. "I stopped by the school to pick you up from cheerleading, and Jade told me you left early. I thought I was supposed to give you a ride," he said, his dark eyes imploring her to explain.

"Oh . . . I wasn't feeling that well, so I caught a ride home with Liz," Tia said, staring down at the floor. "I hung out there for a while."

Angel rubbed at his eyes and shook his head. "So you could have called me from there to tell me I shouldn't come get you."

"I'm sorry. I just forgot," Tia lied, shrugging. Calling Angel had crossed her mind, but the thought of talking to him had made her so ill, she'd been afraid to open her mouth. She lifted her chin defiantly. "What's the big deal? Do I have to tell you every move I make now or something?"

Angel took a step closer. "The big deal," he said slowly, "is that you've been avoiding me."

Tia clicked her tongue. "That is *so* typical," she

162

said, turning away from him. "Everything's always about you, isn't it?"

"What's going on with you?" Angel asked. He reached out for her, but Tia pulled back.

He sighed and put his hands on his hips.

"Tia, you've been acting freaky all week, and then last night . . ." He looked away and bowed his head, as if he was considering his words very carefully.

Tia's heart was in her throat. Whatever was coming, she didn't want to hear it. She just wanted things to be simple the way they'd been two weeks ago. She wanted to go back. Just the thought of the things she'd lost, and the things she was still to lose, brought hot tears to her eyes.

"I just don't get it," Angel said finally, looking her in the eye now. "Everything's fine one minute, and then you run out of my house crying without even telling me what's wrong. And when I called you fifteen minutes later, your mom gave me some line about how you were already asleep and she didn't want to wake you. What's going on?"

Tia exhaled noisily, crossing her arms over her chest. "You want to know what's going on?" she asked, barely holding in the waterworks. "I feel like you don't even care that you're leaving."

"Tia—," Angel started, a definite lecture tone to his voice.

"I'm serious, Angel. You're so excited to get out of here, it's like I don't even exist."

"What?" Angel asked.

"Look," Tia said, "Four days ago I thought we'd be together forever, no matter what. But ever since you got that interview and found out you might be leaving right away, I don't know—it's like you don't even want me anymore. Like you've got more important things to think about or something."

Angel's face was all disbelief. "How can you even say that?" he asked incredulously. "Of course I want you."

"Really?" Tia asked. "Because you didn't exactly jump at the chance to be with me last night."

"Last night?" Angel asked, baffled. But as soon as he had said the words, a kind of recognition seemed to settle into his eyes. "Is *that* what this is all about? Just because I didn't want to have sex with you?"

He might as well have sucked all the oxygen out of the room. Tia almost crumbled at his words. "You said it, not me," she whispered.

Angel rubbed at his forehead. "Tia," he said. "I thought we decided to wait."

"*You* decided to wait," Tia said, narrowing her eyes. "But probably just until you get to college, right? Then you'll probably be ready—for somebody else."

"*What?*" Angel demanded.

"Just admit it," Tia told him. "I don't excite you anymore, but there are going to be tons of women there. I'm sure you'll find someone who can turn you on." Angel's image blurred as the tears took on a life of their own.

"You're not even making sense anymore," Angel said, taking a step back.

"You're just upset because I figured it out," Tia countered, a heavy tear spilling over and hitting the collar of her robe with a plop. "Now you have to admit it's true."

Angel turned away from her and paced halfway across the room and back, stopping in front of her again. "I don't believe this," he said. "After everything we've been through, this is what it comes down to? *Sex?* And not because I'm trying to pressure you into anything. No. You're upset because I love you enough to wait. Do you know how crazy that is?"

"Fine, call me crazy—I don't care." Her face was soaking now, but she refused to choke and sob. "All I know is that last night I wanted to make love with you and you practically laughed me out the door."

He didn't even try to comfort her. Didn't make a move to hug her or even touch her. How could he stand there and say he loved her?

Angel shook his head. "I can't do this right now," he said, sighing heavily. "I've got to go home and pack."

Tia's mind reeled. *Pack? Did he just say—*

"Which reminds me," Angel said. "I just came by to let you know I got the job. They said I was the perfect applicant. I thought you'd be happy for me, but I guess I was wrong. I'm leaving tomorrow."

Tia exhaled sharply. *Yeah, right. This is all about you. Forget the fact that my heart is lying in a lump at your feet.*

But when he turned to leave, Tia was seized by a sudden panic. He'd said he was leaving tomorrow. She couldn't let him go like this. Not with the way things were.

"Angel," she said, trying to catch him by the arm. "Come on. Don't just leave."

"No?" he asked, looking at her over his shoulder. "What do you want me to do? Just stand here and listen to you rant about what a jerk I am all night? I can't believe you'd think this of me, Tia. I can't believe you'd think I could possibly want anybody else."

He swung open the front door and looked at her, his eyes a whirl of confusion, hurt, and maybe even disgust. He was waiting for her to say something. She could see it in his body language—his expression. But she wasn't going to apologize for feeling rejected. Her feelings weren't invalid.

Finally Angel just shook his head and closed the door behind him.

Tia watched from the window, sobbing uncontrollably as he stalked down the walkway and got into his car, slamming the door.

He started to back out of her driveway, then stopped, looking back at the house.

"Come on," Tia muttered through her tears. "Come back."

She watched him and tried to read his thoughts—tried to urge him to get out, walk back into the house, and throw his arms around her.

Suddenly he gunned the engine and peeled out of the driveway. Tia's heart shattered.

They hadn't even said good-bye.

Conner pushed away from his desk as soon as he heard Gary walk into his mother's bedroom. If he was going to do this, he might as well do it Band-Aid style. Quick and painful. He strode through his room and out into the hallway.

Gary had been staying in Mrs. Sandborn's room ever since he had arrived. It had bothered Conner at first—after all, they had a perfectly good guest room—but at least this way he didn't have to share a bathroom with the guy.

Conner reached his mother's bedroom door and raised his hand to knock but stopped, his fingers hovering millimeters from the wood. The door was open a crack, and he could hear Gary talking.

He must be on the phone, Conner thought, more than happy to turn around and put off calling a truce until later. He took a step back from the door.

"I'll be out of here as soon as I can, honey," Gary said.

Conner froze. "Honey?" he mouthed. His stomach

turned over ominously. He couldn't possibly be talking to Conner's mother, could he? Silently Conner leaned closer to the door, cocking his head.

"Look, once I'm done here, I promise I won't let them get in the way again. Have I ever made you feel like you don't come first?" Conner's stomach went from turning to twisting, and he closed his eyes. It definitely wasn't his mother, but it couldn't be what it sounded like. There was no way.

"Sweetie," Gary's voice continued imploringly. "Come on. It's only three or four more weeks. . . . Well, if it upsets you that much, maybe you should come stay here too. There's plenty of room." There was a pause. "Megan? We're getting along great. And if she doesn't like you being here, she'll just have to accept it. I'm her father."

Conner leaned against the wall and clenched his fists, his unkempt nails cutting into the flesh of his palms. He'd almost let himself get sucked in. He'd almost believed Gary was sincere . . . that he might have changed. Conner stared at the closed door to Megan's room, and his heart split open, letting a cold, harsh feeling of disbelief and anger seep out.

How could Gary do this to Megan?

But even worse . . . how could Conner have let himself expect anything more?

At 4:30 A.M. Tia showered and changed, a full two hours before her normal waking time. Her eyes were puffy from crying most of the night, and the bags underneath them refused to be covered even with three applications of concealer. But as Tia climbed into the cool front seat of her mom's minivan, her appearance wasn't her main concern.

Please be there, she repeated in her head, watching the minutes tick by on the dashboard's digital clock. It took at least six hours to get to Stanford, but she didn't know what time he actually had to be there. She did the calculations over and over, praying that Angel hadn't left yet and fighting the sick feeling in the pit of her stomach that told her she'd already missed him.

When she made the turn onto his street, her nerves were completely fried. She would have closed her eyes if she hadn't been behind the wheel. Suddenly Tia noticed some movement down the road, in front of Angel's house.

"Thank you," Tia said aloud. Angel was just closing the hatchback of his light blue Toyota and hugging his mom good-bye. His father was probably at the shop already. He and Angel hadn't spoken much since Angel lost his savings.

Tia steered the white minivan in behind Angel's car and parked. The sound of the emergency brake was loud enough to wake the entire neighborhood in the silence of early morning.

Angel pulled away from his mother's embrace and turned toward Tia's car, freezing as their eyes locked. Tia stepped out of the car and walked slowly toward him. She was shaking, but she never broke eye contact.

Within seconds he'd scooped her up in his arms.

"I knew you'd be here," he whispered in her ear.

Tia pressed her cheek to his. "I'm so sorry," she said.

"Me too," Angel responded, hugging her so tightly that he squeezed out a breath. Loosening his grip, Angel stared down at her. "I love you, you know," he said solemnly. He glanced over his shoulder at his mother, who was standing a few yards away, smiling. "And I *want* you too," he said, lowering his voice. "Nothing's ever going to change that."

"I know." Tia nodded, pulling him close again. "I love you too. And I'm sorry for acting so freaky. I guess I was just scared."

"And now?" Angel asked.

Tia looked up at him with wide eyes. "Still scared," she said with a weak smile. "But not as bad."

Angel kissed the top of Tia's head, and she fought hard to hold back the tears, but they came anyway.

"I've gotta go," he said quietly. Tia nodded as they backed away from each other. Angel stepped off the curb and walked over to the front door of his car, waving one last time at Tia and his mom before getting in.

"It's hard to let him go," Angel's mom said, putting her arm around Tia.

Tia swallowed hard. "Yeah." She listened as he gunned the engine, hit two quick beeps on the horn, and then pulled away, the sound of his motor dimming as the blue Toyota disappeared around the corner.

"Why don't you come on inside and have some coffee?" Mrs. Desmond offered. "You've still got time before school." Tia followed her silently into the house. Just inside the entryway the familiar graduation picture of Angel caught her eye, causing her to smile.

"Bye," she said softly, kissing her index finger and touching it to his lips in the picture. "Take care of yourself."

JESSICA WAKEFIELD
4:02 P.M.

I can't believe I'm going on a date with Will Simmons. Somehow no matter how many times I say it, it doesn't seem real. Unless, of course, I close my eyes, in which case I can still see every detail of his face and feel his lips pressing up against mine. For all I know he asked me out on a date in one of my dreams, but that kiss? <u>That</u> was definitely real.

CONNER McDERMOTT

4:15 P.M.

Megan is going to be crushed.

But maybe that's not totally bad.

The sooner she realizes that everybody lets you down in life, the sooner she'll learn to protect herself.

MEGAN SANDBORN
4:30 P.M.

The truth is, Conner's right. My dad hasn't been the best father. He hasn't always been there for me.

But I don't agree with that whole "people-never-change" thing. People do change.

I mean, Dad's here now, right?

TIA RAMIREZ

4:54 P.M.

ANGEL LEFT TWELVE HOURS
AND NINE MINUTES AGO.
I'VE BEEN (PHYSICALLY) SINGLE
FOR TWELVE HOURS AND NINE
MINUTES.
HOW MUCH IS BUS FARE TO
STANFORD?

ANGEL DESMOND
5:17 P.M.

It's been a long day. I've already seen so much. Done so much. Met so many people.

But I've been seeing Tia everywhere. In the dorm. At the cafeteria. In the bursar's office.

She's never not with me.

And I could never stop loving her or stop wanting her.

She's got to know that's true.

I just hope the same goes for her.